Shayna Gladstone In Search of the Scientist

C.J. Murray

iUniverse, Inc.
Bloomington

Shayna Gladstone: In Search of the Scientist

iUniverse books may be ordered through booksellers or by contacting:

iUniverse
1663 Liberty Drive
Bloomington, IN 47403
www.iuniverse.com
1-800-Authors (1-800-288-4677)

ISBN: 978-1-4502-8990-0 (sc)
ISBN: 978-1-4502-8992-4 (dj)
ISBN: 978-1-4502-8991-7 (ebk)

Printed in the United States of America

iUniverse rev. date: 7/27/2011

CHAPTER ONE
The Prophecy

Shayna Gladstone was so short that everyone in her class at Sir Gawain Elementary School stood at least four inches taller. She was a shrimp next to Trudy Moorphy, who towered a whopping seven inches over her.

At the end of gym class, Mrs. Gangle, a wart drooping below her right eye, reminded the class, "Tomorrow after school we will be holding tryouts for the girls' basketball team. Shayna, you can't try out. We don't have a midget team."

The class erupted with laughter, and Shayna stormed out of the gym.

"Get back here this instant, little lady. I'm warning you!" hollered the warty Mrs. Gangle.

"Sorry, I can't hear you because I'm too short!" Shayna bolted out the doors of the school and scrambled onto her bicycle. She didn't know where she was going, but she was definitely getting away from her bully teacher. She pedaled so hard that her legs seemed a blur.

Shayna wasn't yet across the weedy soccer field before she started to smell bubble gum. The wind picked up and a shadow swept over her. She looked up to see a bizarre hot-air balloon falling from the sky.

"What in the world?" The balloon was headed straight for her!

She tumbled off her bicycle just as the massive hot-air balloon touched down, pinning the wheels of her bike under its basket.

"Holy smokes!" said Shayna, sprawled in a clump of dandelions.

The balloon's shadow blanketed Shayna and half of the soccer field. This was the largest hot-air balloon Shayna had ever seen, easily the size of a schoolhouse.

A winged man, no larger than a groundhog, flew out of the bottom of the balloon and dropped a ladder made of red licorice ropes into the balloon basket. He fiddled at a control panel, whistled a merry tune, and fluttered his iridescent wings.

Overflowing with curiosity, Shayna drew close to the balloon, when she saw a woman shimmy down the licorice ladder sporting turquoise boots with glowing pink laces. Shayna crinkled her nose. Didn't the lady know that her purple and red polka-dotted stockings clashed with the orange bloomers that were hiked up beyond her stomach? The woman jumped from the bottom rung of the ladder to the floor and adjusted the collar of her frilly tie-dye blouse in midair.

"Greetings. I am the Balloon Lady," said the fashion-challenged woman. She straightened the furry yellow fez atop her head and inserted a cardinal feather in the brim. "I hail from Terramanna, the land of fun, frivolity, and merriment. I am pleased to introduce to you our ace scrumption pilot, Atlas of the Skytrak clan." With her index finger, she summoned Atlas, the groundhog-sized man.

Atlas fluttered to the floor of the basket and sprouted to the size of a young boy—a boy with wings, mind you.

Shayna had never seen a scrumption before, let alone one that could fly. "Are you aliens?"

The Balloon Lady burst into laughter. "How fantastic! What a stupendous inquiry."

"Pleased to make your acquaintance, kiddo," said Atlas with a whistling lisp. He bowed and then sneezed in Shayna's face.

Shayna jumped back.

"Ewww." She wiped Atlas's spittle off of her face with her sleeve. "Gross!"

"My friend," said the Balloon Lady, "certainly you know that scrumptions often sneeze on those they admire."

"Uh, isn't that unhealthy?" asked Shayna.

"Don't be silly," said the Balloon Lady. "Sneezing won't hurt him at all."

"No, I meant ... oh, forget it," said Shayna.

"I'm plum thrilled to attend before you," said the Balloon Lady. "I have heard so much about you over the years from our cherished Minnie Maudde."

Shayna blinked her eyes a few times. The name did sound familiar. Then a light bulb went off in her head. "Minnie Maudde, the inventor! You mean my grandfather's cousin, once removed I think."

"Precisely. Not your own cousin. I would never have implied that," said the Balloon Lady. "Frankly, I never intended to come here but after bobbing yon and hither on an exhaustive search for a heroic Shayna, I decided, as a last resort, that I must come to assess your quality of spirit. The Queens' Council dismissed my idea. Afterall, you are merely a child and, as we all know, children can't be involved in anything serious."

"Pardon me?"

"Precisely," said the Balloon Lady. "In accordance with the Constitution of Terramanna, children must have fun, fun, fun. Therefore, you see, matters of importance must be attended to by adults."

"That's absurd." Shayna flipped her sun-bleached brown ponytail off her shoulder.

"Now tell me, my friend, what heroic deeds have you achieved in the name of fun?" The Balloon Lady pulled an oversized notepad and floppy pencil out of a miniature pocket at the side of her bloomers. She licked the nib of the pencil and smiled at Shayna in anticipation of making a note of an outstanding answer. However, when Shayna didn't respond, the pencil became so limp that it folded over on itself.

"I'm a last resort, am I?" Shayna mumbled. "Merely a child? I *am* eleven years old." With those words, Shayna tried to pull her bicycle out from under the balloon basket. The banana seat popped off in her hands, and she rolled backward, landing square on the seat. She blew her hair out of her face with a big huff.

"Marvelous! That was a spectacular stunt. How positively, perfectly fun," said the Balloon Lady. "You are a veritable rib-tickler." She clapped her hands like a circus seal. "Yes, I believe you satisfy subsections one through four of the Prophecy."

"Prophecy?" asked Shayna.

"One: your name is Shayna. Two: you are fun." The Balloon Lady ticked off points in the air with her droopy pencil as she spoke. "Three: you adore candy, gum, treats, and the like. Mind you, who doesn't? And number four: you are destined to save Terramanna."

"What would I know about saving Terramanna?" said Shayna. "I couldn't be the Shayna you're looking for. I know nothing about this Prophecy and I've never heard of Terramanna before. And fun? Do you mean like a clown?"

"You only need come with us to Terramanna, kiddo," said Atlas. "You are Terramanna's hope for continued fun, frivolity, and merriment."

A brilliant question dawned on Shayna. "If I come to Terramanna, will I get to meet Minnie Maudde?"

"Precisely," said the Balloon Lady, balancing her rear-end on the ledge of the balloon basket. She nibbled on the licorice rope. "Yet I confess, my friend, scheduling a meeting with Minnie

Maudde may be a challenge. Nonetheless, in Terramanna, opportunities abound for fun, fun, fun."

"What do you mean, meeting Minnie Maudde may be a challenge?" asked Shayna.

"My friend, it's the fun that's important. Fun, fun, fun," sang the Balloon Lady. "Well, I'm certainly satisfied you are the subject of the Prophecy and that's good enough for me. Now, let's skedaddle to the land of fun, frivolity, and merriment."

The Balloon Lady hopped off the ledge onto the basket floor and handed Shayna a piece of licorice rope.

Shayna flung the licorice around her neck and frayed its ends like a scarf as she stared, deep in thought, at the Balloon Lady. "I want to meet Minnie Maudde. Meeting her is going to be the fun part."

"I'm afraid she's indisposed. Kindly, come into the basket before the balloon departs," said the Balloon Lady.

"Indisposed? What do you mean?"

"She's, well … she's unavailable." The Balloon Lady shuffled her feet and cleared her throat twice.

"Unavailable?" asked Shayna.

"You can't meet with Minnie Maudde because, you see … oh, goodness Shayna, I can't very well simply tell you she's been kidnapped." The Balloon Lady clasped her hand over her mouth. "Oh, pickled peach fuzz. I didn't mean to tell you."

"Kidnapped! That's horrible," said Shayna. "I can't go to Terramanna. It's dangerous."

"My friend, we urge you to reconsider," said the Balloon Lady. "The ancient Prophecy of the Terraman Oracle states that a heroic person by the name of Shayna will restore fun, frivolity, and merriment to Terramanna in the Age of Gloom. The Queens' Council assures us that the Age of Gloom is imminent. I beg you, on bended knee, to help Terramanna defeat unimaginable forthcoming misery."

Shayna swallowed hard. No one had ever begged for her help before, let alone on their knees. This was all too strange.

"Just because my name is Shayna doesn't mean I can do anything about gloom. I'm terribly sorry."

The cuckoo clock watch on Atlas's wrist cuckooed six times. The balloon started creaking and shaking.

"Automatic lift-off engaged," said Atlas.

"Shayna Gladstone!" shouted Mrs. Gangle, marching across the field, pumping her fist in the air. "Little Shayna Gladstone, you get back in the school this minute."

"Hide me!" Shayna jumped into the basket and ducked behind the Balloon Lady. "Please, hide me from my teacher. She always teases me because I'm short. I hate her!"

The balloon made a loud noise like air escaping, and a strong wind whipped up around it. The balloon lifted off the ground, leaving Mrs. Gangle in its wake.

"You get down here this minute, young lady. I'm warning you!"

The balloon rose higher and higher. Shayna peered over the rim of the basket and watched Mrs. Gangle become smaller and smaller until she looked no bigger than a measly ant. The balloon broke through the downy clouds and, at last, Mrs. Gangle faded out of sight.

When Shayna could see nothing but clouds below her, a huge knot twisted inside her stomach. "Oh, no! What have I gotten myself into?"

CHAPTER TWO
The Balloon

"Well, my friend," said the Balloon Lady, "it seems you reconsidered your position. You are on your way to Terramanna."

"I didn't reconsider my position," said Shayna. "I didn't want you to take me away. I just wanted to hide from my teacher. Please turn around and drop me off. My grandfather won't know where I am." The knot in her stomach was now doing back flips.

"Pardon the misunderstanding. Don't fret," said the Balloon Lady. "We are, this instant, dispatching a spectacular candygram to your grandfather advising of your location. I'm quite certain he will understand."

With those words, Atlas released into the sky a mini hot-air balloon with an overflowing basket of glorious candy and a note addressed to "*Grandfather Gladstone, 192 Sterling Street, Urgent.*"

"I want to go home." Shayna pushed her ponytail off her shoulder. "Now."

"You must understand that our destination is pre-programmed with mathematical accuracy to allow us to slip through the International Date Line hole," said the Balloon Lady. "You will be transported back to your grandfather in due course."

"Slip through the what?" asked Shayna.

"The International Date Line hole. You know, the IDL hole. Time warps beyond the IDL hole." The Balloon Lady licked the cloud hanging in front of her face.

"Huh?" Shayna was more than a little confused.

"Oh, my gracious. What do they teach in these newfangled schools nowadays?" said the Balloon Lady. "It's elementary. We merely squeeze through a hole in the International Date Line. Beyond the hole we have three days to every one day on this side of the IDL hole."

"Of course. Elementary. Where is my head these days?" said Shayna.

"Basket up, seal the hatch!" shouted Atlas.

The basket vibrated and moved upward into the balloon, which sealed below their feet.

"It smells like bubble gum," said Shayna.

"Indeed," said the Balloon Lady. "We have a bubble gum factory aboard this fantabulous vessel."

"An entire factory? In a balloon?"

"Come," said the Balloon Lady. She barged through the swinging door of the wicker basket, skipped onto the red and white striped floor, and turned in circles, with her arms swinging about her. Candy sprinkles flew out of her sleeves.

Shayna was awestruck by the kaleidoscopic balloon interior. She arched and leaned back to look at the sparkly purple escalator that spiraled upward to the very top of the balloon. A corkscrewed peppermint stick fireman's pole traveled through the whole length of the escalator. A pit of cushy orange sponge toffee lay at the bottom of the pole.

"Wow!" said Shayna. "I didn't know balloons were like this. How can all this fit in here? And isn't there supposed to be a fire making hot air?"

A deep-voiced scrumption slid down the peppermint stick. "Wahoooo!"

The scrumption hit the sponge toffee pit and did a back-handspring toward Atlas.

"Alvin here hails from the Gomock clan," said the Balloon Lady. "A whole family tree of nuts if you ask me. They adore jokes. Their best gag was when they tricked the fairies into collecting children's lost teeth. Notice that Gomocks have tiny non-flying wings."

Alvin took off his velvet top hat, reached inside, and pulled out a microphone that he placed on a red pillow. Atlas snatched the microphone.

"Attention crew," announced Atlas. His voice echoed throughout the balloon. "Our guest, Shayna of the Prophecy, is now on board. A warm welcoming would be, well, welcome."

Alvin aped Atlas and his echo. Shayna couldn't help but giggle.

Curious scrumptions peaked out from behind seemingly every rounded corner to get a glimpse of the new guest. Their wings smacked together in applause. Some scrumptions were tiny, easily mistaken for bluebirds, and some stood as high as Shayna's shoulders. Yet others grew tall and short without warning.

Alvin plucked things out of his hat. He now had four different hats piled on his head, a rabbit at his feet, and all the while he was tugging a slew of handkerchiefs from his shirtsleeve. His toothy grin never waned.

"Come hither, Shayna; I shall escort you to the Ministry Office to obtain your passport," said the Balloon Lady. "Come now. Time is ticking. Tick tock, tick tock."

Shayna stepped on the escalator with the Balloon Lady. Atlas, now the size of a well-fed northern hare, rode up the escalator, lying on the railing with his arms behind his head, humming elevator music. The escalator carried them upward past seven floors, each floor bustling with activity.

"Atlas?" asked Shayna. "You know how to fly this … this contraption?"

"Sure do, kiddo."

"How does it fly?" asked Shayna. "I mean, it's gotta be heavy with all these people, a whole bubble gum factory, an escalator, and everything else."

"Excellent question!" said the Balloon Lady. "Oh, look. Here's the eighth floor. Our first stop."

The Balloon Lady grabbed Shayna's hand, ushering her off the escalator and through a coiled hallway to a sign on the wall that read "Ministry of Passports, Exports, and Reports." The Balloon Lady fished around in her pocket and took out an ornate doorknob, put it against the wall, and turned it. A door opened to a wood-paneled lobby with marble floors, granite pillars, and a solid brass information desk.

The Balloon Lady stepped up to the desk, behind which a big-winged, spectacled scrumption sat. The scrumption's left ear supported a sticky, chewed pencil that appeared to be a tutti-frutti stick.

"This scrumption is from the Ploomi clan," the Balloon Lady whispered. "Very industrious folk, they are."

The Ploomi handed the Balloon Lady a ticket with the number 102 stamped on it. "Have a seat," he mumbled. The Ploomi stretched his wings and yawned.

The Balloon Lady and Shayna took a seat in lemon-scented bean bag chairs lined up against the wall. Other than the Ploomi, they were the only ones in the room.

The Ploomi, his head down, focusing on paper work, called out, "Number seventy-one."

No answer. Shayna scanned the empty room.

"Number seventy-two."

No answer. Shayna rolled her eyes.

"Number seventy-three."

No answer. The Ploomi continued to call out numbers, clearly in accordance with government policy.

While they waited, the Balloon Lady chitchatted with Shayna. "The scrumptions founded Terramanna long before recorded time. Our notably excellent twin queens, Haspa and Beatrix, govern the region. Terramanna exports many natural resources, including licorice stalks, sun-baked gingerbread, gumballs, chocolate nuggets, maple bricks, vine-ripened marshmallows, and, oh, so many other delicacies."

"Terramanna sounds like a first-rate candy land," said Shayna.

"Indeed."

"But Terramanna is dangerous," said Shayna. "I mean, Minnie Maudde was kidnapped. Who kidnapped her?"

"Precisely."

"Please. Tell me who kidnapped her." Shayna had sunk so far into her bean bag chair that only her head and feet poked out.

"You surely seek answers. Curiosity seems to run in your family. Minnie Maudde herself is a curious sort. But how will knowing that Falco kidnapped Minnie Maudde help you to have fun?" The Balloon Lady's eyes grew wide. "Oh, curdled cream! I've said too much." She slapped her hand over her mouth and zipped an imaginary zipper along her lips.

"Number one hundred and two," the Ploomi called out with his monotone voice.

The Balloon Lady bolted to the desk. Shayna struggled to get out of her bean bag chair. She plopped onto the floor headfirst with her legs split in the air.

The Balloon Lady unzipped her lips. "Good morning, Samosby. Yonder is my newest friend, Shayna Gladstone."

"Is she a contortionist?" asked Samosby.

"Precisely," said the Balloon Lady. She leaned closer to Samosby and whispered, "She seems to be the subject of the Prophecy."

"I do say." Samosby pulled his thick-rimmed glasses down to the tip of his nose and sized up Shayna. "Smallish but definitely not scrumption. Blue eyes like saucers. Eyelashes too big for her own good. Quite a nest of a ponytail. Oh my, she is a mere child."

"I *am* eleven," Shayna said. She swung her matted ponytail off her shoulder. How dare he call her a mere child!

"She requires a passport," said the Balloon Lady.

"Of course. Walk past the identatron." Samosby pointed to a distorted mirror on the wall that appeared to have been confiscated from a gaudy funhouse.

"Oops!" Shayna tripped over her shoelace in an extraordinary fashion and fell in front of the identatron. A mechanical arm appeared from out of the wall, snipped a piece of hair, buzzed, and then dropped a passport in her hands. Shayna opened the cover of the official document, revealing a holographic moving picture of her tripping, a strand of her hair laminated to the page with some sort of chemical composition scribed below, and the pop-up title *Shayna A. Gladstone.* The back cover of the passport had miniscule print that read, "This document serves as your mobile assistant passport (m.a.p.). WARNING: M.A.P.s are not sufficient identification for entrance to Caronstie. Travel to Caronstie is discouraged and is not possible."

"Enjoy your stay in Terramanna." Samosby pulled a window down in front of his desk, apparently from out of thin air. Attached to the window was a sign: "Coffee Break."

Shayna slipped her m.a.p. into her pocket, and the Balloon Lady led her out of the Ministry office. Once in the corridor, Shayna could contain herself no longer. "Who is Falco?"

"Precisely."

"What exactly does that mean?"

"Gracious. What a bundle of questions," said the Balloon Lady. "Kindly accompany me to the bridge."

"Jeesh. You won't take me home because of some stupid hole. I'm trapped inside a weird flying bubble. And you refuse to tell me anything important," said Shayna. "This really stinks."

The Balloon Lady sang old show tunes at the top of her voice as they traveled up the escalator. Shayna didn't recognize the songs, partly because of their age and partly because the Balloon Lady was tone deaf.

The escalator carried them through a cluster of bloated floating red straws. The Balloon Lady grasped two of the long straws out of midair and handed one to Shayna.

Shayna took a sip from her straw, which was almost as long as her body. "Mmmm. A strawberry milkshake!"

"Indeed," said the Balloon Lady. "With a hint of vanilla, a whisper of Bolivian honey, and a soupcon of our secret ingredient: essence of sweet bergamot." The Balloon Lady's hand flew to her mouth. "Oh, green goose livers. I suppose it's no longer a secret."

They got off the escalator on the top floor, number sixteen. Shayna followed the Balloon Lady to a round room with reams of flashing controls and levers. Some of the control buttons were made of jujubes and others of mints.

"Welcome to my bridge, kiddo," said Atlas from his seat at a control panel. He pressed an orange button, and the scent of fresh mandarins permeated the air. The balloon lunged forward, and the lights flashed off and on.

"What happened?" asked Shayna.

"We slipped through the IDL hole, kiddo. We're now moving very fast. About two thousand gigatriptons per twenty IDL minutes. We'll enter Terramanna airspace once we pass over Caronstie." Atlas continued to push, pull, press, and pedal at the control panel. "Make yourself at home, kiddo."

Shayna plopped down in a chair that was the consistency of a fresh marshmallow, a very comfortable chair indeed. A window with butterscotch-scented plaid curtains dropped down from the ceiling.

Shayna slid out of the chair, strolled behind the window, and returned to her seat.

"Atlas, how can I see outside through this window? It isn't against a wall."

"It's an inside window." Atlas continued pushing buttons, pulling levers, and pedaling leisurely. "That chair you're in, kiddo, is the navigator's. He's from the scrumption Timpocki clan.

Timpockis have flying wings, but they like to eat so much that they get weighed down and so don't fly very well. Our Timpocki navigator scooted to the cafeteria for ice cream, double-caramel-dipped maple fudge with a sprinkling of chocolate cherry beans, if I'm not mistaken."

Without warning, ear-piercing clanging sounds erupted.

Shayna covered her ears and shot a look at Atlas. "What on earth?"

"The Caron eagles are in the neutral skyway over Caronstie. They're attacking for some reason," Atlas shouted with a pronounced lisp. "Quick, kiddo, press the Shields button."

Shayna's heart ricocheted off her chest wall. She plunged her hand hard onto the red Shields jujube on the arm of her chair, squishing the button in her palm.

Hideous squawking peppered the air. The noise carried on for six minutes and forty-eight seconds according to Shayna's watch (though that might not have been accurate timing as Shayna's watch lost almost sixteen hours each day). Hundreds of scrawny eagles dive-bombed the balloon. Scores hit the window, knocked themselves out, and plummeted a distance before shaking their heads and flying away.

Atlas pedaled and pushed buttons as though their lives depended on it. The Balloon Lady's hat barely remained perched on her head. She yanked on levers and devoured a cucumber sandwich.

"Strange eagles," said Shayna. She studied the eagles through the inside window and noticed they were flying in formation like the airplanes she had seen with her grandfather at an air show. "Their flying formation looks like a face. Like a man, yes, a man with a beak."

Atlas and the Balloon Lady whipped their heads around to look at the inside window.

"It's Falco. The crest of Caronstie!" exclaimed Atlas.

A blanket of fear settled over the room as a second eagle squadron headed directly for the balloon.

"It's time for the anti-eagle muck guns!" shouted the Balloon Lady.

"Guns!" Shayna couldn't believe her ears.

The Balloon Lady smacked a slew of sticky blue buttons and then a cloud with thousands of strands of tacky cotton candy floss shot from the sides of the balloon. The birds' wings became gummed up with the cotton candy strands, and they broke formation.

The balloon swerved, tossing Shayna from side to side. She grabbed the armrests and accidently hit the soda pop button. A mug of frothy cream soda shot up from the arm of the chair. For the first time in her life, she didn't feel like drinking cream soda.

A loud pop bellowed throughout the bridge, and everyone was thrown to the ground. Air whistled through a ragged hole in the side wall of the balloon. Shayna wrapped her arms around a leg of her chair and felt like her body was a wet dish rag getting whipped from side to side. "Ohhhh, I'm gonna be sick!"

"Puncture!" shouted Atlas. He reached up to the control panel and pulled on the pressure stabilizer lever.

The Balloon Lady ran to the hole and plugged it with her hand. Another loud pop rocked the bridge. Atlas grew as large as a bear, a brown bear to be exact, and plugged the new hole with his hand. Three more punctures erupted, which the Balloon Lady and Atlas plugged with their feet.

"Our shields have failed!" shouted Atlas. "The eagle squadron is too strong. Kiddo, press the manual button and then push the steering square to descend when Lake Orange is in sight. With all these holes, the balloon has slowed enough that you can make a water landing."

"But, I … I don't know how to steer!"

"Precisely," said the Balloon Lady with a sing-song voice as she hung from the wall by her hands and feet.

Shayna had a bullfrog in her throat. The knot in her stomach now sat like an anvil in her gut. She took a deep breath. She had no choice. She had to steer the balloon.

The eagles retreated when the balloon passed over a gulch split in two by a racing river. The pressure of air escaping from the punctures sent the balloon spiraling in wide circles through cloudless sky, beyond a green heath of fragrant spearmint, over red and black fields of ripe licorice, and past a village of candy-colored buildings.

Shayna spotted Lake Orange. True to its name, it was orange and bubbly, like soda pop. She pushed the steering square, held her breath, and the balloon plopped into the fizzy water.

CHAPTER THREE
FIRST TASTE

The crippled balloon bobbed in Lake Orange toward a glimmering white beach.

What a kerfuffle inside the balloon!

Shayna squeezed through the cheering scrumptions on the escalators while being sprinkled with gumdrop confetti. She was soaked by a steady rain of sneezes.

"What's all the cheering for? It's a little embarrassing," said Shayna to the Balloon Lady.

"You're a celebrity," the Balloon Lady shouted to Shayna over the din of the crowd. She held a spittle umbrella over Shayna's head.

"A celebrity?" asked Shayna.

"Come, my friend. We have drifted to the incomparable Sugar Beach."

Shayna jumped out of the basket onto the beach, catching her foot on the rim of the basket as she exited. She sprawled face-first onto the sand. When she looked up, her face was covered with white powder.

"Wow! I never expected this." Shayna licked her lips. "The beach is made of sugar!"

"Please pardon my haste," said the Balloon Lady. "I must attend the Queens' Council meeting and advise them of your arrival. Remember, Shayna … fun, fun, fun!"

In a whiff, the Balloon Lady was gone.

Shayna felt abandoned. What could she do other than hang around the balloon and wait to go home?

Shayna watched scrumptions drag the tattered balloon onto Sugar Beach, and the knot in her stomach grew. With so many rips in its hull, the balloon looked like it had flown through a tornado. How would she ever get home?

Atlas flew about the exterior of the balloon, examining the damage. Every time he saw a hole in the hull of the balloon, he clicked his tongue, "Tsk. Tsk. Tsk."

Beyond the balloon, a team of synchronized swimming Gomocks, each wearing purple nose plugs, splashed in Lake Orange. They were god-awful synchronized swimmers. In fact, they were so bad that, at first, Shayna thought they were practicing drowning.

"*Mon dieu*. They are terrible," said a raven-haired girl standing nearby. She flipped her sunglasses onto the top of her head. "But they are much fun to watch, yes?"

"Uh, yeah," said Shayna. "Fun."

Shayna couldn't help but stare at the girl's big arm muscles. And she was almost as tall as Trudy Moorphy!

"My name ees Marie." The girl held out her hand to greet Shayna. She had a strong grip highlighted by calluses on her palms. Each of her fingernails had tiny candies painted on them.

"I'm Shayna. Hey, I like your accent."

"Really? I usually get made fun of because of eet," said Marie. "I just moved 'ere last year from Quebec City with my mother."

"This place is … different, isn't it?" asked Shayna.

"Ah, *oui*. I thought so when I first moved 'ere too. But eet ees very fun," said Marie.

Marie studied Shayna. "Um, there was a rumor that a person named Shayna would be coming 'ere. Are you … oh gosh, I might as well just ask. Are you Shayna of the Prophecy?"

"Prophecy? You know about that?"

"Hey, Marie, kiddo," yelled out Atlas. He zipped up to the girls. "Shayna is here all alone. Why don't you two celebrities hang out together until I can get my balloon repaired and get Shayna home?"

"Sure. I would love to!" said Marie.

Marie grabbed Shayna's arm and pulled her along a path made of rock sugar that led to a forest. At the edge of the forest was a sign: "Gumball Grove."

"I want us to go to 'ypogeal Park. I 'ear the park ees *formidable* but 'ard to get een. Come on, Shayna. I 'ave never been there. Eet will be fun."

"Sure," said Shayna, elated that someone as tall as Marie was willing to hang out with her. She had to wait for the balloon to get fixed anyway.

Shayna trekked with Marie through Gumball Grove and bonked her head on peculiar gumballs that seemed to dangle from every tree. Red and blue gumball juice stained her forehead each time she whacked her head on one of the strange fruits.

"Gumballs don't grow on trees," said Shayna. A monstrous gumball fell on her head. "Ouch!"

"They do een Terramanna." Marie plucked a handful of ripe gumballs off a tree and shared them with Shayna.

"Are you a celebrity?" asked Shayna. She blew a bubble the size of a melon. It popped, and colorful rainbows escaped.

"'Ardly." Marie laughed with a snort. "Atlas only said that because I am a sneak for one of the Terramanna rafters teams. Atlas ees one of our coaches, my favorite. The championsheep tournament ees tomorrow. Of course, I will be more famous when we win. But I will never be as famous as you. I mean, I am not een any textbooks." *Pop* went her gum.

"Textbooks?" *Pop*. More rainbows.

"Oui. Yes. You are Shayna of the Prophecy, are you not?"

"I don't know." Shayna spit out her gum in a hollowed out stump labeled "Gum Scum." "I don't even know what the Prophecy is."

"Oh, but the queens say eet ees the Age of Gloom. The rumor ees that someone named Shayna …"

"Do me a favor, Marie. Don't spread that rumor." Shayna tossed her ponytail off her shoulder.

"Your wish ees my command." *Pop.*

Beyond Gumball Grove was a network of tree houses supported by a stand of gnarly gumball trees with arched doorways carved into their trunks. The area was teeming with people lolling about in the shade at the Gathering Stump, an outdoor lounge of huge proportions set below the tree houses.

Some people were snoozing in over-stuffed nutshell recliners. Others played ping-pong with coconut macaroons. Shayna and Marie passed under the canopy of one of the larger trees where a group of Timpockis were staging a boisterous competition to see how many pecan pies they could each fit in their shoe pockets. Whole pies magically disappeared into shoe pockets without any trace. A handsome boy judging the competition caught Shayna's eye.

She stopped in her tracks. She knew she was staring at the boy, but she couldn't help herself—there was something different about him. She could have gawked at him all day if Marie hadn't interrupted.

"'Ere. Try this." Marie snatched an enormous fizzling gumball from a barrel and tossed it to Shayna. "These are my favorite."

Shayna struggled to stuff the gumball in her mouth, which made Marie laugh so hard that she snorted. Shayna laughed at Marie snorting.

"Sorry," said Marie with another snort. "I always snort when I laugh 'ard. I cannot 'elp myself." *Snort.*

Shayna held her stomach and laughed harder. *How funny is that … a girl who snorts!*

Shayna contorted her face, trying to shove the gumball in her mouth again. She stopped when someone tapped her on the shoulder. It was the boy who had been judging the disappearing pie contest.

"You'll never get it in your mouth that way," he said.

"'ello, Dan," said Marie. She turned to Shayna. "Dan ees on my rafters team, Shayna."

"Shayna?" Dan asked.

Marie nodded. "She ees new 'ere."

Dan winked at Shayna. He had one green eye and one blue eye. Shayna melted.

Dan took the gumball from Shayna and put it in a paper bag. "It's called a gumplosion ball. Watch this."

Dan whacked the gumplosion ball on the ground.

BANG!

He gave the bag to Shayna. Peeking inside, she saw that the giant gumball had imploded into hundreds of small gumballs, just the perfect size for popping into her mouth.

"Mmmm. Sour and sweet," mumbled Shayna while chewing on a mouthful of gumballs. "Bubbly."

"So, you must be Shayna of the Prophecy," said Dan.

Shayna shrugged. She couldn't say anything with her mouth so full of gum.

Shayna blew an outstanding bubble that was green with purple dots. Finally, when the bubble neared the size of a small pony, it popped. The force of the explosion sent Shayna reeling into the barrel of gumplosion balls, causing the spilled gumplosion balls to split into rolling heaps of gumballs. A mist of rainbows spewed from the barrel.

"Impressive," said Dan.

Nearby, a clock chimed twelve times. The crowd at the Gathering Stump stopped all games and raced to a thick hollow tree trunk. A sign floating in midair at the trunk doorway flashed "Porker's Pizza." The smell of oven-fresh pizza wafted on the breeze.

"Pizza's ready," said Dan. "It's always ready when the perpetual clock chimes at noon."

Dan pointed to a tower clock located on a peppermint patio just beyond the Gathering Stump. The clock was made up of gadgets and gears. Gobstoppers were plunking loudly at set intervals onto a teetering maze of peppermint circuitry. With each chime of the clock, the smell of peppermint overpowered the scent of the pizza.

Dan continued his timely lecture. "Perpetual clock's been running accurately now for five hundred and eighty-seven years. The only fixing it ever needed was some butter once when the hands got creaky."

A gaggle of twelve-year-old girls sauntered in high heels toward Dan. Each girl had long silky hair, pouty lips, painted nails, and dressed in foolishly tight miniskirts. The leader of the pack stopped in front of Dan.

"Hey, Daniel," said the pompous girl. "Join us at Porker's Pizza for some cheesenut pizza."

"Not now, Christie. I'm gonna hang out with Marie and Shayna, if that's all right with them," said Dan. He winked at Shayna.

Shayna smiled and nodded in agreement.

Christie eyed Shayna from toe to head and smirked. "*This* is Shayna? Shayna of the Prophecy? She's so … so short. And dirty. Look, ladies, Prophecy Girl's got gum juice all over her."

The gaggle of girls crowded around Shayna and laughed.

"She ees not dirty," said Marie. "You are 'orrible to say that."

"Blah, blah, blah," said Christie. "Nobody can understand your dumb accent, Frenchy." Christie pushed Marie aside and stood nose-to-nose with Shayna. "I don't like you, Prophecy Girl. You think you're so great just because of the Prophecy. The stupid Prophecy isn't true. Soon you'll see that the Prophecy is wrong and Falco will make you pay big time."

Christie and her clan wobbled away on their high heels toward Porker's Pizza, laughing.

"How dare you treat my friend like that!" yelled out Shayna. "And how dare you say those things to me!" With those words, Shayna slipped on a gumplosion ball and landed on her derriere. She gasped for air.

Christie and her clan snickered and pointed at Shayna as they walked in the direction of Porker's Pizza.

"What does she mean, Falco will make me pay?" asked Shayna.

"Forget about it," said Dan. "Christie just likes to make trouble."

CHAPTER FOUR
A Mounce

"To find your way around Terramanna, you can look at your m.a.p. Go ahead. Look for Hypogeal Park," said Dan.

Shayna pulled her m.a.p. out of her pocket and flipped it open. Shayna saw her holographic moving picture pinpointed on the m.a.p. at the Gathering Stump.

"Oh, here I am." She was excited to find her location and even more so to see her moving picture on the m.a.p., even though her picture kept tripping.

Dan explained, "Your m.a.p. is personal to you. Only your voice will activate it. If you ask your m.a.p., it will also remind you of special events, like rafters tournaments, popcorn volcano explosions, and the balloonport schedule. Occasionally I can get it to do my homework for me too. It does everything."

"Brilliant," Shayna said.

"So, if you want to find a place, just tell your m.a.p.," said Dan. "Go ahead; tell it."

"Mr. Map," Shayna shouted with the m.a.p. up close to her lips, "please tell me how to get to Hypogeal Park."

Instantly the m.a.p. lit up a path from Shayna's picture, along Watermelon Way, over Cake Walk, beyond Maple Forest Terrace, and stopped at Hypogeal Park with a loud *ding*.

Shayna and her two new friends ran along Watermelon Way, following the path set out on the m.a.p. The street abutted the fragrant Candy Sprinkles Desert on one side and narrow watermelon fields on the other. This contrasting scenery was not only startling but also an inexplicable environmental absurdity. In the first field were gleaming white watermelons. In the next were blue watermelons, and in the final field were purple watermelons. The ripe watermelons made heartbeat noises, their skins expanding and contracting with each beat.

"I've never seen anything like that," said Shayna. "Is this kind of abnormal stuff normal in Terramanna?"

"Abnormal?" said Dan. He shrugged. "I don't know what you mean."

The friends sauntered along Cake Walk, a sweet-smelling street made of different kinds of cakes. Shayna found the fruitcake best to walk on because it was hard and dry, rather like department store fruitcake.

Beyond Cake Walk, Dan pointed out the maple tree forest that bordered Maple Terrace. "Those are ever-flow maple trees, genetically engineered by a famous scientist," Dan explained. "The trees produce sap all day, every day, all year. Anyway, the scientist that engineered them is a genius. She's been the chief scientist in Terramanna for years. Rumor is that she disappeared about a month ago, which is a tragedy 'cause I was looking forward to the regenerating potato chips she invented. I read that they are one-foot-wide potato chips that regrow with each bite. You'd only ever need one potato chip. Then *poof!*" Dan snapped his fingers. "Just like that, she disappeared before the final testing."

"That scientist must be Minnie Maudde," said Shayna. "She's my grandfather's cousin, once removed, I think."

"Minnie Maudde ees your cousin?" asked Marie.

"She's not my cousin. I would never imply that," said Shayna. "Minnie Maudde is my grandfather's cousin."

"Gosh. You 'ave very famous family."

"Really?" said Shayna. "I never knew."

The friends stopped at a flashing Hypogeal Park sign that floated above a doorless gingerbread hut. The hut was decorated with gumdrops, candy corn, and swirly lollipops. Blue frosting icicles dripped from the eaves. It looked a lot like a big version of the gingerbread house Shayna made with her grandfather at Christmastime.

"This is Hypogeal Park?" asked Shayna. "For some reason I pictured it much bigger."

"This is just the entrance," said Dan with a know-it-all tone. "Obviously, the park is underground."

Marie picked up a doorknob from a bucket of screaming doorknobs and placed it against the wall. Nothing happened. The doorknobs yelled, "Try Me! Try Me!" It was quite a racket, each doorknob attempting to yell louder than the rest.

The trio sifted through the doorknobs, trying each one against the wall.

"Look," said Shayna. She turned a sparkling crystal doorknob against the wall and fireworks went off inside the knob. "Finally, we found the right doorknob!"

The door swung open into a gigantic lobby where a fountain of hot fudge flowed down one wall from ceiling to floor. Fancy carved pillars of glimmering rock candy adorned the lobby. Strawberry plants balanced on the lip of the fountain such that the tip of each berry lay dipped in the hot fudge. Pear trees grew at the sides of the fountain, allowing the fruit to hang in the rich chocolate.

"This room is definitely a big mounce," said Dan. He snacked on a fudge-dipped pear.

"What's a mounce?" asked Shayna. She nibbled on creamy hot-fudge-covered strawberries. Delicious.

"A mounce is a structure that is larger on the inside than the outside due to a warp in space. The scrumptions know how to trap mounces. They split mounces into little bits and make shoe pockets, bottomless pit pockets, purse pits, and that kind of stuff. I've read that there are really big mounces in Terramanna. But, other than the rafters tunnels, I've never seen a big mounce."

At the far end of the lobby was an open elevator manned by a dainty lady scrumption, a Skytrak, who was no larger than a parakeet. Her fluttering wings glimmered with iridescent blues and pinks, which complimented her uniform.

"All aboard for Hypogeal Park," announced the scrumption. The friends entered the elevator. The scrumption pulled an imaginary cord above her head, a train whistle sounded, and the elevator dropped into the ground.

When the elevator opened to Hypogeal Park, the friends were in the middle of a discussion.

"But how do you know that it was Falco who kidnapped Minnie Maudde?" asked Dan.

"The Balloon Lady told me by mistake," said Shayna. "She also accidentally told me the secret ingredient in the strawberry milkshake straws."

Marie and Dan exchanged worried looks.

"What? Is it bad to know the secret ingredient?" asked Shayna.

"Falco is the king of Caronstie," said Dan, as if Shayna should know these things. "People say he's half man, half bird. He's evil, a really mean dictator. And I bet I know why he kidnapped Minnie Maudde."

"Why?" Shayna and Marie asked simultaneously.

"Listen," Dan whispered, "I heard, well, I eavesdropped on the Balloon Lady talking to Samosby in the Ministry office a few days ago. She said steps need to be taken to prevent invasion by Caronstie. I thought she was joking. But last month there was also an article in the *Sweet Read* newspaper that reported threats from

Caronstie. I'll bet that Falco wants Minnie Maudde to invent something to destroy Terramanna."

"Oh, gosh," said Marie. Her knees wobbled.

The scrumption elevator operator had been listening in silence, until now that is. "It's really happening."

The three friends jumped, having forgotten that the scrumption was present. The scrumption's wings whirred so fast that they were barely visible. "It's the beginning of the Age of Gloom. May the Prophecy save our souls." She took her cap off and held it over her heart.

The elevator doors slid shut leaving Shayna, Marie, and Dan standing at the gateway to Hypogeal Park.

Shayna looked back and forth between Marie and Dan. "And I'm supposed to stop this invasion somehow? I'm supposed to stop gloom?"

"According to the Prophecy, yes," said Dan.

"I can't stop any invasion," said Shayna, her eyes welling with tears. "I want to go home. I miss my grandfather."

"But the Prophecy says ..." Dan's sentence trailed off as he saw a tear drop down Shayna's cheek. He couldn't stand to see girls cry. "As soon as we've seen Hypogeal Park, we'll take you to the Balloonport so you can sign up for a flight home."

"Will you leave too? I mean, if there's gloom ..."

"No. I belong here. Besides, how could I leave a place like this?" Dan motioned to the spectacular subterranean view before them. "Look at all the everglow rock. You'd think it was daylight, but we're over nine hundred feet underground."

A glowing green rock passageway led to a lush heath with flower gardens and ponds. Next to one pond was a small sign: "*Pony Fish Rides*." Marie ran to line up in the cue, eager to ignore any worries about the Age of Gloom. "I 'ave always wanted a ride on a pony fish."

"Oh, look!" said Dan. "Newt races!"

He ran to the stadium-sized newt-racing oval with Shayna trailing behind him. At the racing oval, oversized smelly newts pulled miniature golden chariots commandeered by tiny yet plump Timpockis. Dan rooted for Slip Slide, a huge orange newt with bulging red eyes.

"Slip Slide has such good breeding," he explained to Shayna, raising brass binoculars to his eyes.

Dan seemed to get lost in this newt-racing world.

Many ladies in the crowd topped their heads with wide-brimmed hats, like Eliza Doolittle's, and pushed to get better views of the races. Shayna couldn't care less about smelly newts, so she left to explore the rest of the park by herself. After all, she was supposed to have fun, and stinky newts simply weren't fun in her book.

Every ride or activity was crowded. Shayna found only one ride without a cue, the Jungle Ryde Tour. A rustic sign, draped with climbing plants, directed Shayna down a dirt path, behind a thorny hedge, to an everglow rock boulder. Ivy stretched in both directions along a wall.

Shayna jumped onto the everglow rock boulder only to find that it was moist and slippery. She fell directly into the ivy wall … or rather right through it.

"Ooof!" exclaimed Shayna as she landed on her duff. When she picked herself up, she was surprised to see that the wall of ivy was actually a wall of glass covered by ivy on the other side. On this side, however, the wall of glass was shiny and bright, like diamonds. It stretched endlessly to the left, to the right, and up to where it disappeared into the canopy of the jungle, where she now found herself.

The only opening in the glass was where she had just fallen through.

"Holy moley!" Shayna exclaimed as she stepped up to take a closer look. The glass wall was thicker than her arm was long. But at this spot, it had been smashed, creating an opening just large enough to fit through without getting all sliced up on the jagged edges.

A sudden *honka honka* noise made Shayna spin around. A rusty yellow bus with the words "Jungle Ryde Tour" smeared on the side clunked to a stop in front of her, spitting smelly black smoke out of its exhaust pipe.

CHAPTER FIVE
JUNGLE RYDE TOUR

The doors of the dilapidated bus creaked open. Shayna got on the bus to find herself alone with the driver, a gangly, mostly toothless, bespectacled (broken nonetheless), stubby-nosed man who smelled of expired cottage cheese. The bus doors banged shut behind Shayna.

The man grunted, "Sit where ya want, kid. Just gotta get me tape recorder rollin'."

He gunned the engine and pressed the Play button of a primitive tape recorder with his bony forefinger. The bus puttered into the jungle.

A taped voice introduced the driver. "Welcome to the Jungle Ryde Tour. Your driver today will be Boobie Schumpert."

Shayna giggled at the mention of the driver's name.

"Somethin' funny, runt?" the man asked as he glared at her through the rearview mirror.

"Well, actually your name is funny, Mr. Schumpert," Shayna replied between fits of giggles.

"I already knows it's funny. Boobie Babee Bummer Schumpert. What was me parents thinkin'? But ya shouldn't be laughin'. Laughin' gets ya in all sorts o' trouble in these here parts."

Shayna would have gotten off the bus right then and there if it weren't already moving. She sat four seats behind Boobie Schumpert and examined the back of his head while he drove. His hair was patchy, ashen brown, and oily. His skin was like a shedding snake's.

"Mr. Schumpert," said Shayna. "I like your name. I'd be proud to have a name like yours. My name just seems to be getting me into all sorts of predicaments lately."

"You don't know the half o' it, kid."

The muffled tape-recording started again. A pleasant tour guide voice lectured, "We are now entering the deepest, oldest, and only subterranean jungle on the planet. It spans five thousand three hundred and forty-eight hectares. In this jungle resides every snake known and unknown to man. Keep all windows closed and plug any and all holes in the body of the bus with fiberglass resin."

The farther they ventured into the jungle, the darker it got. Shayna was soon sweating from the heat. Massive venus fly traps were snaring unsuspecting rodents by the side of the road. The larger venus fly traps even snapped at the bus.

The road was bumpy and likely not a road at all judging from what could be seen in the dim headlights.

The driver lit up a putrid cigar. Cigar smoke hung like mini storm clouds in the thick air.

It was so dim Shayna could only see outlines of trees and plants and, uuuuggggh, two-headed snakes slithering along the hood of the bus. Huge, thick snakes.

A din of hisses grew louder and louder until it seemed snakes surrounded Shayna. And, in fact, they did … on the outside of the bus. Shayna plugged her ears with her fingers, but the hissing still oozed in. One snake coiled itself so tightly around the bus that it dented the roof.

As they drove on, the hissing subsided, allowing Shayna to take her fingers out of her ears.

She hacked from the gritty cigar smoke and cracked open her window to get some fresh air.

The sappy recorded voice warned, "Keep a look-out for the fascinating blue-barred stinging beetles. They gather in troupes of one hundred and forty-eight to twelve thousand and ninety-six individuals. Troupes are easily identified by a thunderous stampeding noise. This tour bus may retreat into a subterranean bus shelter should a stampede occur. You can expect to meet your demise should the bus be unable to take refuge from these impressive stampedes."

She looked out the driver's window and found that her eyes were now adjusting to the dim light. She saw cinnamon-haired monkeys swinging from branch to branch. Some clung to the side of the bus.

Boobie Schumpert raised his fist at one monkey that sat on the side mirror, picking his nose and smearing it on the glass. The brave creature raised his snotty fist in return.

Because Shayna watched the monkey business on the outside of the bus, she failed to notice a spider monkey had entered through her window and perched on the backrest next to her shoulder. When she turned, she was greeted with a gnarly-toothed grin from the primate.

"Aaaargh!" she screamed so loudly that the bus driver slammed on the brakes, causing all the monkeys dangling from the side of the bus to be thrown to the ground. Shayna fell to the floor and crouched with her arms covering her head.

The smelly man got out of his seat, sauntered past Shayna, closed the window, and locked it. He stood over her. "It's just a wee monkey. He ain't never hurt no one," said Boobie Schumpert, holding the monkey like a baby.

Shayna dared to look up and was instantly smitten. "He's soooo cute. He really likes you, Mr. Schumpert."

He handed Shayna the monkey. "Ain't no one never called me mister before."

"Why not? It's respectful," said Shayna, still cooing over the little primate and scratching it behind the ears.

"Respect?" said Boobie Schumpert. "I ain't never imagined that." He returned to the driver's seat and fell deep into thought as he started up the bus again.

The tape recording continued, "Primates, such as spider monkeys, squirrel monkeys, gorillas, and gibbons are common residents of this jungle."

The monkey cuddled up next to Shayna as though he had found his long-lost mother. "I'm going to name you Monkey Doodle. That's a fun name. Mr. Schumpert, what do you think about naming him Monkey Doodle? Is it funny enough?"

"Monkey Doodle. Yeah, Monkey Doodle is a good one. It's more stupid than funny," said Boobie Schumpert. "It ain't a name likely to get no laughs. Won't hurt him none."

"You're just jealous you didn't think of it," said Shayna, flicking her ponytail off her shoulder.

The cigar smoke was now so thick that Shayna had to wave it out of her face every couple of minutes. And, as might be expected, monkey see, monkey do.

Without any forewarning, a mad rhinoceros impaled the side of the bus with his horn. Shayna gasped and jumped sideways to avoid the sharp tip. Her tongue was tied with fear. Her heart pounded against her chest wall.

The bus engine slowed to a rickety idle as the rhino heaved the bus off the ground and tossed his head from side to side. Boobie Schumpert remained calm and kept revving the engine as though the bus was stuck on ice. Monkey Doodle jumped up and down, screeching, taking breaks from these fits only to clean his fingernails on the sharp tip of the horn of the beast.

Eventually, when the rhino tired of tossing the bus around with his horn, Boobie managed to drive back onto the road.

"Holy cow," said Shayna, looking out her window at the beast. "He's still stuck to the side of the bus with his horn."

"He ain't no cow," said Boobie.

Suddenly, Shayna heard a rumble and the ground shook. The bus squealed off the road, dragging the rhinoceros with it. The bus skidded to a stop in a pitch-black underground cave. The rumbling noises from above grew to deafening proportions. Monkey Doodle crawled up to Shayna's neck and hid under her ponytail, where he shook like a leaf, as did she. Shayna thought she might faint from fear.

The scaly man puffed on a cigar, his fourth since the tour began. The only light came from the tip of the smoldering cigar.

"Big troupe o' blue-barred stinging beetles o'erhead," the driver hollered. He seemed delighted to have uninterrupted time to puff insatiably on his rank stogie.

The thunderous noise diminished within minutes. The bus pulled out of the shelter. A few beetles were wandering about, trailing far behind their troupe. The beetles ranged in size from a teacup to a toilet.

The bus ran over and squished at least three beetles, each of which let out a yelp before their brown guts spewed across the jungle floor. Shayna held her breath and almost vomited from the crunching sounds.

She gathered her senses and, in a weak voice, said, "I'm not having fun. Can we please go back now, Mr. Schumpert?"

The driver slammed on the brakes, causing Monkey Doodle to tumble off the seat, Shayna to sail down the aisle on her stomach, and the rhinoceros to dislodge from the bus.

"Back? No! Yer the only kid who's ever taken this tour," yelled Boobie Schumpert. He glared at her as rancid cigar smoke billowed from his lips and curdled in the air. He marched to her, lifted her to her feet by the collar, and shouted in her face, "This ain't supposed to be fun. This is supposed to be me ticket outta the dungeons."

"I want to leave now!"

"Join the crowd!" yelled Boobie Schumpert.

Monkey Doodle drew his ears back and squealed.

Shayna broke free and pushed the bus doors open. She raced out of the bus. Shayna feared Boobie Schumpert more than the blue-barred stinging beetles. However, her freedom was short-lived. Within seconds, a snare vine snagged her leg and snatched her into the canopy of the jungle, dangling upside down. "Aieeee!"

"Quit yer whining," said Boobie to Shayna from below. "It's just a snare vine."

"I'm not whining," Shayna shouted. "I'm screaming!"

"Monkey Doodle," Boobie called out. "Get up that there tree and unsnare her if ya knows what's good fer ya."

Monkey Doodle did as told, and Shayna plummeted into Boobie's bony arms, knocking Boobie out of the path of a sow-sized blue-barred stinging beetle. The beetle kicked up his rear feet and charged. Shayna pulled Boobie to his feet and into the bus. Boobie tugged the door shut and rushed to plug the rhino horn hole with some gray goop from a bucket under his seat.

He coughed up yellow sputum on the floor next to the driver's seat and flicked on the tape recorder, which made whirring noises as it got up to speed. The crazed man restarted the bus and drove on.

"Thanks, little friend," Shayna yelled through a window to Monkey Doodle.

The bus slowed and sputtered to a stop. Boobie looked back at Shayna in the cracked rearview mirror. "How come ya says Monkey Doodle is a friend?"

"Because he's nice to me," said Shayna, glaring at Boobie Schumpert. "Monkey Doodle and I have that in common. And he doesn't do things to scare me, like another person I know who shall remain nameless, if you know what I mean. And he risked his safety and got me down from the snare vine, unlike the same other person I know who shall remain nameless, if you get my drift."

Boobie sat quietly, his brow furrowed. Then he erupted with excitement. "I guess that means yer me friend. Ya bin nothin' but nice. Ya called me mister. Respect? I ain't never had it, 'til ya said so. And, ya like me name. Ain't nobody else likes it. And ya got a name that gets ya in trouble too. That's in common, ain't it?"

Shayna nodded out of courtesy, not knowing what to make of Boobie.

"Then ya goes and saves me by riskin' yer hide fallin' accidentally on me. Ya got me outta the path o' the beetle and saved me life, fer what it's worth. That makes ya me own friend, don't it?"

Shayna smiled politely. She was petrified of him but felt sorry for him all at the same time.

Boobie revved the engine and continued the tour.

The trees thinned, and they approached a grassy savannah abounding with wildflowers and butterflies. Shayna thought this sight might actually have been pleasant had it not been tainted by the heavy cloud of cigar haze and the terror that still swelled in her gut.

"Mr. Schumpert, if you were my friend, you'd take me back now," said Shayna.

Boobie Schumpert drove on in silence.

The pesky tape-recorded voice interrupted. "Often giralephants can be spotted grazing the plains. Note their pachyderm-like trunks are the exact same length as their long necks. These gentle-natured giralephants are endangered, as are the less genial razor-back hinks that are certainly observing you and planning a gory attack. However, due to their narcoleptic nature, hink ambushes are often unsuccessful."

Shayna could not see any giralephants or, thankfully, razor-back hinks. She was happy for their narcoleptic nature, whatever that meant.

The wannabe road led the spent bus into the Dead Jungle, an eerie and lifeless stretch of land.

The cheery tape-recorded voice carried on, "The Dead Jungle is replete with the remains of many lovely animal and plant species, including the extinct three-legged hairy grabbot. Note the stunning lifeless trees and vines."

"I wanna be yer friend," said Boobie, oblivious of the scenery. "I ain't never bin one." He blew his nose in his sleeve.

What Shayna saw from her window wasn't pretty. Animal skeletons littered the jungle floor. Maggots smothered trees. Fungus the size of large platters drooped from lifeless trunks. Wizened vines dangled between dried-out tree branches and formed a canopy so dense that only a spattering of light seeped through. A stagnant stream snaked among the decaying trees and ended at a motionless brown cesspool.

The only sounds came from canary-sized Kamikaze mosquitoes splattering against the windshield. Green goo dripped down the windshield with every gargantuan bug that suicided by flinging itself at the bus.

An erratic, winged creature swooped from the sky and nabbed one of the mosquitoes in mid-flight. A bat. A monstrous bat.

Swarms of bats dive-bombed the bugs at lightning speed. Their sonic squeals pierced the dank air. Shayna hated bats. She hated them even more than blue-barred stinging beetles. She squeezed her eyes tight and plugged her ears with hopes that this would all end soon.

Boobie Schumpert stared at Shayna in his rearview mirror. "I'm takin' ya back now," he said. "I can't do this to ya. Yer me friend." He wiped his nose on his cuff.

The recorded voice went on. "There are many species of bats in this jungle, including the mutated Kittie's hog-nosed bat, the Malayan flying fox, and the infamous Vampire bat. Some bats feed on insects, others on fruit, and still others on blood."

Boobie pressed the Fast Forward button on the tape recorder and it sped up the recorded voice to a high-pitched screech.

Thoughts of the bats occupied Shayna's mind until finally the pitiful bus sputtered to rest at the bus stop beside the glass wall.

"This ends the Jungle Ryde Tour. If you have survived your excursion, we look forward to seeing you again." The nauseatingly sweet recording stopped, and the tape recorder button clicked off.

The bus door creaked open. “Good-bye, Mr. Schumpert,” shouted Shayna as she dashed from the bus. She didn’t dare look back.

“Good-bye, me friend,” said Boobie.

Shayna bolted through the ivy-covered hole in the glass wall and sighed, relieved to have made it out of the jungle in one piece. The ivy closed over the jagged hole behind her, leaving no trace of its existence.

CHAPTER SIX
STRANDED

Shayna raced to the elevator without seeing any of the fun parts of Hypogeal Park, like the rock lobster concert, the electric eel light show, or the gelatin trampolines. She wanted out of Hypogeal Park and out of Terramanna. She wanted to go home.

"Whoa," Dan said as he grabbed Shayna's arm. "Where did you go? We couldn't find you anywhere."

Shayna was out of breath and holding her side. Stale gray cigar smoke wafted from her nostrils with every breath.

"What 'appened?" Marie asked. "You look 'orrible and smell even worse."

Shayna plopped onto the floor of the elevator. She was exhausted. Dan and Marie stood at each side of her.

"All aboard," announced the scrumption manning the elevator. Again, she pulled an imaginary cord overhead and a train whistle sounded. The doors to the elevator slid shut.

Once outside the mounce, Shayna blurted every detail of the Jungle Ryde Tour to her two friends.

When Shayna described the squishing of the beetles, Marie closed her eyes and grimaced like she had just eaten a rotten egg. Dan didn't feel sick until Shayna described the monster mosquitoes splattering on the windshield.

"No one has ever told me about the Jungle Ryde Tour. I've never even read about it," said Dan. "I don't know why something so dangerous would be in Hypogeal Park. You could have been killed."

"You've never heard about the ride because I'm the only person who's ever gone on it," said Shayna. "No offense, but this place isn't fun at all. I want to go home."

"But it usually ees fun," said Marie. "I wish you would stay. And not just because of the Prophecy."

Shayna sighed. Tears welled up in her eyes, but she refused to cry. She missed her grandfather so much right now that she felt like screaming.

"Don't worry," said Dan. "We'll take you to the Balloonport to sign you up for a flight home." He winked at Shayna, which somehow made her feel better.

Dan and Marie led Shayna past Caramel Cove, along Spearmint Street, beyond the rafters launch and the Hatching Fields, past several ritzy boutiques and the licorice farms, until finally they neared the Balloonport. Here they noticed a huge crowd had formed. Weeping erupted from near the front of the crowd, along with bits of frantic conversation.

Atlas flew overhead along with Queen Beatrix's royal assistant, a pudgy Timpocki dressed in velvet robes, who was having trouble staying in flight. He was posting notices on trees.

"Atlas, what ees 'appening?" Marie shouted through the crowd.

Atlas dipped down from the sky while the royal assistant continued on his way, bobbing up and down above the throng of people.

"Good news and bad news," said Atlas, his lisp pronounced. "My balloon is repaired but the crest of Caronstie is in the skies at all times now. Falco has officially declared war. The minister of War and Peace and Fine Literary Works has ordered that all balloons into and out of Terramanna are canceled until further notice."

"But I want to go home!" Shayna exploded.

"Until this war is over, we can't fly over Caronstie. And that's the only way to the IDL hole. Sorry, kiddo. You're stranded." With those words, Atlas whizzed away.

Shayna felt like a truck had fallen on her. "I've got to get home," said Shayna. "I have a math test on Monday. Mrs. Gangle will fail me if I'm not there. I have gymnastics practice on Tuesday. And I miss my grandfather." Tears hung at the edges of her eyes.

A massive troop of eagles flying in the formation of the crest of Caronstie formed a black cloud over the cliffs of Caronstie.

"Why would Falco declare war?" said Marie. "We did not do anything to Caronstie."

"I read a book from my godfather that said Falco believes that fun is the great crime of the civilized world. In Caronstie, public laughter and celebrations are crimes," Dan said. "The book said Falco would destroy Terramanna and all our fun if given the chance."

Shayna stared at the crest of Caronstie and began to seethe hatred for Falco. "He's kidnapped my relative. He wants to destroy Terramanna. And he's making it impossible for me to get home." Shayna turned to her friends. "We have to do something."

"I wish we could, but the constitution won't allow anyone under sixteen to do anything except have fun. Just ask your m.a.p. It can explain the constitution to you," said Dan. He walked away from the noisy mass of people. "I'm sure the Queens' Council will think of some great invention to defeat Caronstie. After all, Terramanna is much smarter scientifically, especially when Minnie Maudde is chief scientist. She'd come up with some invention that would win this war."

"You think she could find a way to get me to the IDL hole?" asked Shayna.

"Yep," said Dan. "She can figure out anything."

"Well, then that does it," said Shayna. "We'll just have to rescue Minnie Maudde."

Dan and Marie looked at each other, worried.

"If we don't get her back, Falco will make Minnie Maudde create things to destroy Terramanna. Then I might never get home," said Shayna. "Oh, no! He could do terrible things to her. He could torture her or … or worse. We have to rescue her."

"Shayna, be realistic. We are too young," said Marie. "We cannot simply march over to Caronstie and get 'er back."

Shayna focused on Marie's accent, trying to understand her, and walked straight into a tree, knocking herself to the ground. She blew her hair out of her face.

"Besides, everyone in Terramanna knows that there's no way into or out of Caronstie," said Dan, sticking his hand out to help Shayna up.

"If there's no way in or out of Caronstie, then how did Falco get into Terramanna to kidnap Minnie Maudde?" asked Shayna, her hands on her hips and eyebrows raised.

The question hung in the air. No one had an answer.

CHAPTER SEVEN
The Hatching Field

"Shayna, I do not like to think about these kinds of things. Kidnapping, war. Eet frightens me. We should leave eet to the adults," said Marie. "Dan and I 'ave rafters practice. Come watch. Eet will be fun."

Shayna trudged alongside her friends without saying a word. She paid little attention to the path they took until her friends stopped walking. She looked to both sides of the street. On the left was a flashing neon sign: "Rafters Launch." On the right was a field filled with the strangest, most colorful eggs Shayna had ever seen. Hundreds of scrumptions were closing in on the field from all directions: with wings or odd flying contraptions, even on hummingbirds.

"Oh, *bon*!" said Marie, eying the eggs in the field. "A 'atching ees about to 'appen. Shayna, you 'ave to stay to watch. Oh, darn eet. I wish we could stay too. You are going to love the 'atching."

Shayna watched the hustle and bustle of scrumptions in the field and sighed. "Really, Marie. The only thing I'd love right now is to go home."

Before she knew it, a scrumption had dropped a shiny white pot with blue silk lining into her hands. "Crackpot," said the scrumption as he shuffled Shayna onto the field. Shayna looked back to find her friends, but they were gone.

Shayna had no idea what a hatching was but was soon caught up in the hubbub and felt awestruck by the organized chaos. Everyone was having so much fun.

"Over here," hollered the Balloon Lady, waving Shayna toward her. Atop the Balloon Lady's floppy yellow hat were three peacock feathers. She wore a tuxedo-tailed shirt with red sleeves and a pink rhinestone bodice. Her orange skirt fluttered in the wind.

Shayna tip-toed through the eggs and sat on the grass next to the Balloon Lady. The commotion was enchanting and overpowered her thoughts of the war.

"Greetings, my friend," said the Balloon Lady. "So much ado for our sixth hatching this season. I do adore the hurly-burly. You?"

"Yes. I guess … I guess I do too," said Shayna. "But, I don't know what a hatching is. What's going to happen?"

"Jumping jellybeans! Do you mean to tell me that this is your first hatching? Ever?"

"We don't have hatchings like this on the other side of the IDL hole," said Shayna.

At that moment, loud cracking noises resounded throughout the field.

The Balloon Lady lifted her finger as though a grand idea had popped into her head. *Crack! Crack!* She raised her arms and a green peppermint baton ejected from her sleeve. She began waving the baton as though conducting an orchestra.

Then Shayna saw it. One of the blue and gold polka-dotted eggs before her trembled and cracked. A wet, sticky gingerbread man cookie burst out of the egg and fell to the ground, where it dried in the sun. Shayna got on her belly and examined the spilled contents of the egg. She poked it with her finger. Suddenly, right next to Shayna, another cookie burst from a shiny red egg, then another from a green egg with blue swirls, and then from a yellow egg with pink dots. The eggs burst about her, spewing eggshells in the air, forcing her to keep her eyes tightly shut. Eggs throughout the entire field exploded with gingerbread men, all of which sprawled on the grass and hardened in the sun. The harmonized cracking sounded like a symphony. Pungent smells of gingerbread lingered in the air.

Shayna, with eggshell stuck in her hair, picked up a hardened gingerbread man. "These hatch from eggs? Huh. Go figure."

"It's the freshest method. Baked in the sun, never overdone," the Balloon Lady said. She munched on the arm of a dried gingerbread man. "Simply divine."

Shayna nibbled on a cookie. "Holy crow. These are amazing."

Scrumptions buzzed about, collecting gingerbread men in crackpots. These pots were obviously mounces because many more gingerbread men went into the pots than would mathematically fit.

By the time Shayna finished eating her third cookie, her excitement waned and her thoughts again turned to going home. Despite the grand event unfolding around her, Shayna could think of nothing more than rescuing Minnie Maudde. She knew that Minnie Maudde would find a way for her to get home. And what if—oh, how Shayna hated to think about this—what if Falco were forcing Minnie Maudde to create inventions to destroy Terramanna? What would Falco do if Minnie Maudde refused? What would Falco do if she agreed?

Far in the distance on the Caronstie cliffs, Shayna could see a castle with towering turrets blanketed with dense gray fog. A black cloud of eagles, which formed the Crest of Caronstic, circled over the castle, occasionally disappearing from sight into the fog.

She realized that the castle must belong to Falco. To test her suspicion, she asked, "Does Falco live alone in his castle over there?"

"It's no secret that many servants live there too," answered the Balloon Lady. She tilted her head and became solemn. "Shayna, I know why you're inquiring about the castle. However, by confidential ordinance of the queens, I am not permitted to tell anyone that Falco is likely keeping Minnie Maudde at the castle." The Balloon Lady repeatedly hit her forehead with her palm. "Oh, mushed mangos. I can't believe I told you that."

"Minnie Maudde is at the castle! We have to rescue her!"

"No, no, no. There is no *we* involved. A rescue effort is a very complex adult matter," said the Balloon Lady while juggling three gingerbread men. "Under no circumstance are you to try to enter Caronstie. In the past, others have tempted such fate and have died." She stopped juggling and looked Shayna in the eye. "You would certainly be killed trying."

"Killed?" Shayna gulped. "How?"

"Along the Zyluss River and its tributaries to the north are two-hundred-foot cliffs of crumbling rock," said the Balloon Lady. "Try climbing and you will fall to your death. That is, if the caron eagles don't get you first. They would simply eat you alive." The Balloon Lady bit the head off of a gingerbread man.

"Halfway down the river, the rapids commence. If you commandeered a boat, you would be thrown into the acid water and your body would smash over the caustic waterfall. Of course, if the caron eagles didn't get you first.

"If you found a way to traverse Cackle Creek to the west without being sucked under by the groping algae, you would find yourself smack dab in the middle of the scorpion breeding ground. You would be attacked by hundreds of stinging scorpions and that would be the cause of your demise."

"If the caron eagles didn't get me first, right?" Shayna said with her head hung.

"Ah, I see you're getting the idea," the Balloon Lady said. "Now, to the east, beyond the Popcorn Volcanoes, is a treacherous canyon. Though it is passable by skilled outdoorsmen, you will find a crowded cactus field on the other side. The cacti have poisonous heat-seeking thorns that would certainly simmer your blood and cause a prolonged, painful death. Hundreds of eager caron eagles patrol that area too.

"Beyond the cactus fields, one would find a sinking sand desert, known as Dead Man's Cross, and that meets up with Blackwater Lake to the southwest. Blackwater Lake is filled with thick hot tar. You cannot cross it because you would stick to it and burn. And, of course, the caron eagles will make a meal of you while Falco watches and cheers."

The Balloon Lady's serious demeanor instantly changed. "Yet, as a youthful prophetic figure, I understand your desire to help. I would expect no less. The Queens' Council has determined that you can assist with the recovery of Minnie Maudde in a singularly significant manner."

Shayna scooted to her knees. "How? How can I help?" Finally, someone, the Balloon Lady of all people, understood her need for Minnie Maudde to be returned to Terramanna.

"Come hither. I will tell you," whispered the Balloon Lady, peering side to side, making sure no one was listening.

Shayna shifted until she was nose-to-nose with the Balloon Lady. She felt she might explode with excitement.

The Balloon Lady smiled and said, "You, my friend, can have fun, fun, fun!" The Balloon Lady shot to her feet, clapped her hands, and jumped up and down, turning in circles as though she had just been awarded the most astounding prize in the universe. Jelly beans sprayed from her sleeves.

Shayna's shoulders slumped. She couldn't believe that the Balloon Lady had suggested this. It was nothing, thought Shayna. She was to do nothing.

Shayna's knee slipped on a wet gingerbread man and she fell forward, bonking her forehead on the ground. She didn't care that it hurt.

"I don't see how doing nothing will help," said Shayna.

"Oh, for the love of cake. Fun is not nothing. It is fun!" exclaimed the Balloon Lady.

"It's not much of a plan."

"Precisely," said the Balloon Lady. "Understand, my friend, fun is miraculous. With fun comes joy and laughter. Creativity abounds. Health is enhanced. Friendships blossom. Fun powerfully enriches all lives. We are trusting that you can summon fun in Terramanna during these difficult times."

"I don't see how having fun will help," Shayna said. She pulled her ponytail tight.

"Gracious, I must find out what schools are teaching these days. The answer is obvious. The fun, frivolity, and merriment exuding from Terramanna positively affect the moods and thoughts of neighboring countries. Fun is a far more powerful force than despair," replied the Balloon Lady. "If Falco can't drum up enough despair, despondency, and depression in his subjects, he will be unable to make them invade Terramanna. That fact is undisputed. Who wants to fight when they could be having fun? Enough said. Have another cookie."

After other pleasant conversation and a few more gingerbread cookies, Shayna and the Balloon Lady left the Hatching Field and went their separate ways, Shayna to the rafters launch and the Balloon Lady to, well, wherever the Balloon Lady goes.

CHAPTER EIGHT
THE M.A.P.

When Shayna approached the rafters launch, Dan was standing by a pile of massive donuts. Atlas dragged a donut to the top of the launch, which steeply sloped into the Honey River. Donning a green and blue helmet and life jacket, Dan ran full speed along the runway at the top of the launch, jumped into his donut bottom first, and slid down the mogul-riddled launch. He plucked a sugar cane paddle from the overhead paddle grab at the bottom of the launch and headed toward a tunnel.

Atlas shouted instructions through a bullhorn, "Keep your bottom out of the water, kiddo; straight like a board. Hold your paddle tight in case rafts come up behind you." His whistled S's were exaggerated with the amplification from the bullhorn.

Dan disappeared into the tunnel. If Shayna didn't know the tunnels were a mounce, she'd have wondered what could possibly take so long to go such a short distance. Atlas buzzed around, pacing in midair near the tunnel exit.

Atlas shouted a few more directions through the bullhorn as Dan emerged from the tunnel, paddling hard, and heading for the winding rapids. He dropped over a sugary waterfall and crossed into Lake Orange. Dan raised his arms into the air. Atlas gave two thumbs up.

From the top of the lifeguard tower where she sat, Shayna could see Falco's castle. Through the mist she spotted dark clouds of birds patrolling the Caronstie skies. The crest of Caronstie hung in the skies as a reminder of the war. Shayna's heart sank. She wasn't convinced that simply having fun would be enough to end the war, save Minnie Maudde, and get home.

Shayna was brought back to the present by the sound of a bugle. A Timpocki, wearing a burgundy bowler hat and green pants with gleaming suspenders, raced around in circles on a ruby-throated hummingbird while blowing a bugle. He stood on the bird in flight and announced, "The evening feast is set! Wahooo! Only one-half hour until our taste buds meet heaven."

The hummingbird-riding Timpocki whizzed in front of Shayna and stopped on a dime, hovering in the air at her eye level. "Miss Gladstone? Shayna of the Prophecy?" the Timpocki asked.

"Yes. Or, no. Well, maybe," Shayna replied.

"Maybe schmaby. Silica P. Nightshade I am. Sandy, for short." He sneezed at Shayna with both eyes wide open. "I apologize for being star-struck but I have looked forward to this moment for a long time."

Sandy let go of the reins of the hummingbird, snapped a picture of Shayna, and bowed like a Victorian gentleman, even tipping the bowler hat. He gave a loud, "Yahoooooo!" and then zipped away on the hummingbird.

Shayna shook her head. How strange was that?

She was suddenly very excited about dinner and, in fact, hungry enough that she put aside thoughts of Minnie Maudde. She ran along the riverbank to Dan and Marie, and slipped on the wet grass. She rolled backward in a straddle position and privately thanked her grandfather for putting her in gymnastics lessons. As she popped to her feet, the only evidence of her tumble was the grass stain splotched on her back.

"Hi, you guys," said Shayna. "I watched you go through the tunnel, Dan."

"It's quite a maze in there. Hey, team," Dan shouted, "This is my friend, Shayna."

The team crowded around Shayna. Some insisted on talking as if to impress her, and others remained distant, apparently awestruck by her presence.

"Who's your favorite rafters team?" asked a muscular boy of about fourteen years of age.

"Our team, the Riff Rafts, of course," Marie cut in.

"Of course," said Shayna. She tossed her hair off her shoulder with a whip of her head.

"Do you know much about rafters?" asked a girl with flaming red hair.

"Well, the donuts look really tasty," said Shayna.

The rafters laughed again, some more than the comment warranted. Shayna curled her ponytail around her fingers. She felt odd surrounded by so many people who wanted to talk to her. This never happened at home.

"You see, there are nine people on each team: a stopper, a recoverer, three blockers, three sneaks, and a finisher," Marie explained and pointed out the people on her team who held each position. "The stoppers launch first and they must race through the tunnels to the exit to stop finishers from other teams getting out of the tunnels. Only stoppers and finishers can make physical contact. Sometimes the, uh … the word ees sparring, between stoppers and finishers can get very nasty at the exit.

"Recoverers provide supplies. They 'ave to be strong to carry everything. The blockers block members of other teams from getting through the tunnels."

"I'm a blocker!" yelled a stocky boy trying to get Shayna's attention.

"You're a block head," said Dan.

Marie snorted and continued. "Then there are the sneaks. I am a sneak. We try to trick other rafters eento taking tunnels that are either slow, low een water, or dead ends.

"The finishers 'ave to get past everyone to get to the finish line."

"So, basically the finisher has to ride a donut on water through tunnels," said Shayna, "get past the blockers and the sneaks, and then fight the other teams' stoppers on the way to the finish line."

"That ees the short version of the rules, oui."

"Team, pack up and have a fun dinner. And quit crowding Shayna," said Atlas from the riverbank as he piled the donuts into a wheelbarrow.

Marie invited Dan and Shayna to dinner with her at Pumpkin Patio.

"Eet ees my favorite restaurant een all Terramanna," said Marie.

Shayna had never gone to a restaurant without her grandfather before. He always paid. Shayna didn't know what to do. She had less than three dollars in her pocket.

"I don't think I can go," said Shayna. "I don't have any money to pay for dinner."

"Wow, you really don't know much about Terramanna, do you?" said Dan. "You don't need money in Terramanna until you're sixteen. Everything is free for kids." He snickered as though he couldn't imagine someone not knowing that.

Shayna blushed with embarrassment. "How would I know? I've never been here. I'm sure there are lots of things you don't know about where I live." She didn't mean to raise her voice but it just came out that way.

"Sorry, you're right." Dan winked at Shayna, and she forgot why she had gotten huffy.

"You can practice with your m.a.p. and ask eet to direct us to Pumpkin Patio," said Marie to Shayna.

"You don't have to yell at your m.a.p. like last time, though," said Dan. He yelped as Marie jabbed him in the ribs. "I was just sayin' …"

"Please, Mr. Map, show me the way to Pumpkin Patio," said Shayna.

Ding! It displayed her picture, with arrows along the route to Pumpkin Patio.

As they followed the m.a.p.'s directions, Shayna asked, "What's with your team? Why were they all so … so all over me? It was a little weird."

"Oops, sorry about that," said Dan. "I kind of mentioned that you were Shayna of the Prophecy."

"Dan! You were not supposed to say anything," Marie said.

"I didn't know. I'm sorry," said Dan.

"I feel like you're hanging out with me just because you think I'm someone famous," said Shayna.

"No. No, it's not like that. Well, m-maybe at first. But not now. I really like you. I promise I won't brag to anyone else that you're *the* Shayna."

"Good," said Shayna. "And I don't want any more people snapping pictures of me like that nut on the hummingbird."

"Oh, mon dieu," said Marie, lapsing into her native tongue. "Dan, you told your godfather about Shayna?"

"Sorry, I didn't know I wasn't supposed to. He came to announce dinner when I'd finished my run through the tunnels," he said. He turned to Shayna, "And, by the way, Sandy is not a nut."

"No? He took a picture of me while he was standing on a hummingbird," Shayna said. "None of this matters anyway because everyone seems to think I'm Shayna of the Prophecy. Even Christie thinks so. But I don't want you to be my friend only because I'm supposedly *the Shayna*."

"From now on," Dan said, "I'll think of you as just Shayna … period. And maybe you can think of Sandy as not a nut."

"Ooh la la!" squealed Marie as Pumpkin Patio came into sight. "There ees a table overlooking the pumpkeen patch."

Scrumptions carted food to the table on silver platters the instant all four were seated. Shayna had never seen a spread like this, even at Thanksgiving. There was roast beef and fluffy Yorkshire pudding smothered in smooth brown gravy, two-foot-long butter-dipped cobs of corn, super-stretched spaghetti with chunky tomato and garlic sauce, and pancakes so light that they floated a couple of inches above the table until drenched with gooey maple syrup. There were also cherry chunks in blue coconut shells, flambéed cheese on sesame crackers, and milk in three-foot-high goblets. The strangest thing Shayna ate was throbbing watermelon salad, which felt like fruit doing the polka as it went down her throat.

The bowls and plates were made of cookie wafers and tasted as great as the meal itself. The knives and forks were crafted of tasty rock-hard sugar.

As the evening set in, Gomocks went from table to table, entertaining guests. Some Gomocks did magic tricks, like turning potatoes into weasels or pulling carrots out of people's ears. One Gomock inserted a raw cob of corn into one ear and pulled a cooked buttered cob out of the other. No one ate that cob.

Shayna said, "I think that trick would be better with waxed beans."

Snort.

"So, I spoke with the Balloon Lady at the Hatching Field," said Shayna as she took a bite of marshmallow toast. "She says I'm just supposed to have fun. She said if it's fun in Terramanna then Falco won't be able to force his troops to attack."

"Fun does have a certain charm," said Dan between bites of asparagus dipped in whipped cheddar.

"She says rescuing Minnie Maudde is an adult matter," said Shayna.

"Well, I think the Balloon Lady ees right. Besides, we do not know where Minnie Maudde ees."

"Yes, we do," said Shayna.

Shayna's friends stopped eating and looked up at her.

"The Balloon Lady's not so good at keeping secrets," said Shayna. "She told me that that she isn't allowed to tell me that Minnie Maudde is in the castle on the cliff."

"The castle. Oh. Well, eef they know she ees een the castle they must 'ave a plan to rescue 'er."

"All I know is that the Queens' Council's plan for me is to sit back and do nothing but have stinkin' fun."

The three friends, who were the last patrons remaining at Pumpkin Patio, sat quietly eating their dessert: a mouthwatering five-layer caramel mousse cake garnished with chocolate antlers and vanilla bean sauce. In the distance, beyond the Candy Sprinkles Desert, and by the light of the sunset, they watched hot-air balloons near the Caronstie cliffs getting tangled in their own candy floss webs. Other balloons crossed beyond the Caronstie cliffs but retreated from the army of attack eagles when their efforts to lure them away with birdseed torpedo cookies failed. Two balloons hit each other with candy floss, which resulted in one of them floating sideways through the sky in a tangled mess. Three other balloons spiraled through the sky when punctured by eagles. One narrowly missed crashing into the Zyluss River.

Dan broke the painful silence. "I don't think it matters if you are Shayna of the Prophecy or not. We can't just sit here and leave this to the adults. We have to rescue Minnie Maudde. Look at those balloons. Falco's likely laughing his beak off right now. This is so embarrassing."

"We cannot rescue Minnie Maudde. What about the constitution? I will not break the law. My mother would be mad at me."

"It wouldn't be breaking the law if we had fun while rescuing Minnie Maudde, would it?" said Dan.

"That is so smart!" Shayna jumped to her feet.

"Just one problem, smarty-pants," said Marie. "No one knows 'ow to get eento Caronstie."

Shayna had a sudden bout of brilliance. She pulled her m.a.p. out of her pocket and wiggled around like she had to use the toilet. "Mr. Map. Pretty please, show me how to get into Caronstie."

The m.a.p. went wild with arrows pointing in various directions and then backtracking over and over. Her picture kept tripping and tripping and tripping.

"Ooops, I think it's stuck." Shayna banged it on its side like it was a broken television.

"I should have told you not to ask that," Dan said. "If it can't find a place it'll search for hours and then give up, exhausted. It'll refuse to communicate with you for days or will purposely point you in the wrong direction to get back at you. That happened to me once when I tried to trick it. Boy, was I sorry. You're going to be without a m.a.p. for a while."

"Moldy marshmallows. I thought it would work!" said Shayna.

CHAPTER NINE
Sweet Suites

The three friends walked past the Hazelnut Forest, beyond Scrumption Stadium, and along Hickory Crescent (or as Marie said, "'Ickory Croissant").

Marie stopped in front of a sprawling Victorian style house. "'Ome sweet 'ome. Gracious, eet ees nine o'clock already. I need lots of sleep for our tournament. Dan will take you to your 'otel, Shayna. See you tomorrow, mes amis." Marie waved and went in her house.

"Well, if my map can't show us how to get into Caronstie, we have to find a way ourselves," said Shayna. "Can't we sneak in with a small balloon late at night?"

"Eagles are on patrol twenty-four seven," said Dan. He led Shayna along Nougat Street.

"There's a way," said Shayna. "I know there's got to be a way."

Soon Shayna found herself standing across the street from a glitzy skyscraper set amongst a tangle of trees. The branches seamlessly flowed into and out of the building. The network of tree houses entwined in the branches would be unnoticeable if not for the soft light filtering from their windows.

Splat! Shayna was soaked with water.

"Okay. Who did that? Show your face so I can pound you!" yelled Shayna.

She looked up to see Christie standing on an ornate second-floor balcony jutting from the massive trunk of a neighboring tree. Midnight-blue curtains fluttered in the balcony doorway.

"Oh, my goodness," Christie said with feigned innocence. "I was out here looking at stars and just happened to drop my drink. What a shame. I was thirsty."

Christie leaned on the balcony rail. "Daniel, I'm surprised a star like you is hanging out with Prophecy Girl. I'll save your reputation and walk you to your tournament tomorrow." Christie gave Dan a pinky finger wave and disappeared behind the curtain.

"When donkeys fly," said Dan under his breath. He turned to Shayna as though the incident with Christie had never happened. "Before you are the Sweet Suites, the best hotel condos in all of Terramanna. I suppose this is where you'll be staying. Sandy and I live here in the Whipped Cream condo during the school year. We live in our cottage at Caramel Cove during school breaks."

Shayna twisted her ponytail to wring the water out of her hair. "How come you don't live with your parents?"

"They died in the scorpion breeding ground when I was two."

"Oh, I'm sorry," said Shayna. "My mom disappeared when I was a toddler. And then my dad died in an accident right after that. So I live with my grandfather."

"You miss him?" Dan asked.

"Yeah. A lot. He's all I've got." She took a deep breath and suddenly realized why she had been bewitched by Dan from the first time she saw him. "I never met anyone else without parents before."

"We're special." Dan winked at Shayna.

For the first time in her life, Shayna felt like someone understood. It was a comfortable feeling, an intimate feeling.

Dan opened the frosted glass doors to the lobby of Sweet Suites. Shayna stepped inside and fell speechless. The lobby had a green everglow rock floor etched with delicate pictures of famous scrumptions. The floor cast a comforting light upward through the canopy of tree houses. Orange trees, grape vines, banana plants, and native caramel bushes with tasty brown buds grew from the floor of the lobby. Gilded gold walls housed children's art, which was hung with the honor usually reserved for great artists.

Dan picked two candy daisies out of one the edible flower arrangements that adorned tables carved from compacted cocoa powder. He handed one to Shayna, and she nibbled a white petal. Mmmm! It tasted like a lollipop.

"Your m.a.p. would tell you what room you're in," said Dan, "except you've put it into a loop."

Dan pulled his crumpled m.a.p. out of his pocket, and when he snapped it open, it was perfectly flat with not a single crease. "What room is Shayna Gladstone registered in?"

He smiled and showed the m.a.p. to Shayna. "Mmmm," said Shayna. "I'm in the Chocolate Condominium. Oh! I get a whole condo?"

"Chocolate is right next to our condo," said Dan. "I don't remember anyone ever living in it so it'll be like new. Follow me, neighbor."

They picked up a doorknob at the reception desk, and then Shayna followed Dan to a massive tree with turreted mansions suspended in its branches. Dan opened a door into the trunk of the tree. Shayna followed him down a circular staircase. Stained sugarglass windows pebbled with gumdrops lined the stairwell.

The lights along the walls of the stairwell were made of huge acorns. Chipmunks had taken up residence in the stairwell and were greeted by Dan as though a part of the family.

The two exited the trunk halfway up the tree through a large arched doorway onto a tree branch mezzanine.

"Uh, wait a minute," Shayna said, rightfully befuddled. "We went down the stairs. How did we get up this tree?"

"It's an optical illusion. All tree stairwells are like that," Dan replied in a know-it-all manner.

"To your left is your condo," said Dan. There was no door but Shayna could smell chocolate so she knew they were close. Shayna felt relieved to have a place to stay near a friend. She put the doorknob against the wall and turned it.

"Drop by my place in the morning for Sandy's famous game-day waffles," said Dan. "Sandy's expecting me home now. Gotta go."

Shayna pushed her door open and was overwhelmed. She had never smelled anything so decadent. Most furnishings were a calming milk chocolate hue. There was a movie screen, message hub, and games center that extended the full length of the far wall.

She checked out the master bedroom. The four-poster king bed was humungous. The bedposts looked like they were carved from logs of dark chocolate. On a whim, she licked one. Yep … chocolate.

Shayna peeked around the corner into the cocoa-wood-paneled library. The library was stacked with leather-bound books housed on shelves behind glass doors. Shayna examined books bearing many delicious titles, including *Cheery Chocolatiers*, *Chipping Chocolate*, *White vs. Dark Chocolate Debates*, *Calculus for Chocoholics*, and even *The Belgian Chocolate Lab*. A desk and navy blue wing-backed desk chair sat against a wall of windows overlooking the lights of the Terramanna shopping district, Lake Orange, and the cliffs of Caronstie.

"Sweet," Shayna said aloud. She thought to herself how much her grandfather would love this view and then was overwhelmed with the stabbing pain of homesickness.

"Minnie Maudde, I need you," said Shayna, looking toward the cliffs of Caronstie. "I need you to help me get home."

Shayna stepped back into the master bedroom when the cuckoo clock on the wall chimed ten o'clock. A little wooden man dressed in Austrian mountain garb poked out from the small hole above the twelve.

The wooden man yawned. "Welcome home," he said. "Bedtime." He tossed into the air a single chocolate truffle wrapped in blue foil. The truffle smacked Shayna on the side of her head.

"Hey, what's the big idea?" She picked up the truffle from the floor, unwrapped it, and took a bite.

"Oh … my … goodness. This is the best thing I've ever tasted in my entire life."

Shayna opened the chest of drawers at the foot of the bed and was delighted to see that it was filled with fashionable clothes in her size.

She changed into red pajamas, and as she sat on the bed, she caught sight of herself in a full-length mirror. The mirror shouted, "Brush your teeth!"

Surprised, she slipped off the edge of the bed and fell with a distinct *thunk* to the floor. She didn't dare look in the mirror again before brushing her teeth.

Shayna awoke the next morning at six o'clock as the cuckoo clock man littered the floor below his clock with breakfast treats. "Time for fun," chimed the wooden man every time a treat plunked on the floor.

After putting on new blue jeans and a funky green shirt, Shayna checked herself out in the mirror. "Brush your hair," shouted the mirror.

"Whatever," said Shayna. She brushed her tangled hair and stuck it in a ponytail.

Ding!

The noise startled Shayna. "Oh, my m.a.p.!" She turned yesterday's pants upside down and the m.a.p. fell out.

"No way! Awesome!" said Shayna as she examined her m.a.p.

Shayna ran out of her condo to Dan's door, or at least where she thought the door might be. She knocked on the wall, and an eyehole flicked open. Sandy, who now stood as tall as Shayna, threw open the door and greeted her with a sneeze.

Dan's suite was all white and fluffy, like whipped cream. The condo was huge, and the pale hardwood hallways off the living room seemed to go on forever. Dan sat at the kitchen table, gorging on waffles smothered in exploding blueberries. The white table was spotted with blueberry juice.

"Good morning," said Shayna. "What a beautiful day."

With a toss of her hair, she signaled Dan to come out into the hallway.

Dan jumped out of his chair and quickly muttered, "Uh, Sandy, I'm taking Shayna around this morning. See you at the tournament!"

Shayna tugged Dan out the door into the mezzanine.

"Check this out!" Shayna laughed and did a jig as she tossed her m.a.p. to him.

Dan stared at the m.a.p., his eyes wide. Eventually he lowered the m.a.p. "I guess I was wrong. I honestly didn't think the map would know how to get to Caronstie. But I'm not sure it's right. I mean, it points to the rafters tunnels. I've been in those tunnels hundreds of times. I've never seen any kind of entrance to Caronstie."

"Have you ever known any m.a.p. to be wrong?"

Dan crinkled his brow. "No, m.a.p.s are always right. Unless they're playing a trick on you, but you'd know it's a trick. This is definitely not a trick. Let's find Marie and ask her if she's ever seen anything in the tunnels."

Dan and Shayna raced to the spinning umbrellas at the Gathering Stump. Shayna gobbled up dragon fruit slices and a honey apple muffin offered by a fly-by tympocki waiter.

Marie was sitting under a yellow and purple spinning umbrella, sipping on Fruit Pow energy juice. A feast of peach slices, fresh bread, apple butter, and vegetarian bacon sat before her, untouched. A scrumption wearing an apron put a frothy orange smoothie on the table and flew away. The smoothie changed color every few seconds.

Marie was engrossed in the morning edition of the *Sweet Read*. Dan picked at Marie's food.

"Listen to this," Marie said as she slapped Dan's hand away from her food. "The Queens' Council 'as posted armed guard balloons along the Terramanna border at the Zyluss River to dissuade possible eagle incursions eento Terramanna. Guard balloons are armed with anti-eagle muck guns, 'igh-powered liquid sugar blasters, Gomock joke bombs, and peanut brittle. Nightly fireworks displays on the banks of the Zyluss River will celebrate Terramanna's commitment to fun."

"Joke bombs? Peanut brittle?" asked Shayna. "Does the Queens' Council think that will end the war? Insane."

"Gomock joke bombs are really fun," said Dan. "But, then again, they are dangerous. They affect the central nervous system. In fact, in 1842 a joke bomb was tested in the Bran Desert. It turns out that an entire tribe of nomads living at the edge of the desert had to be hospitalized because their stomach muscles cramped when they got the giggles and couldn't stop. Then, in 1991—"

"Arghhh. No 'istory lectures today," said Marie.

"Hey, Marie," said Shayna. "Have you ever seen any strange passageways in the rafters tunnels?"

"Pardon?" Even this small word carried a touch of Marie's accent.

Shayna opened her m.a.p. on the tabletop. Marie studied it and said, "Eet seems 'ard to believe. But, then again, I 'ave not been een every tunnel. We 'ave got to tell Atlas."

"Marie, we can't tell anyone about this entrance to Caronstie or they'll close down the tunnels. Our tournament will be canceled," said Dan.

Marie looked back and forth between Dan and Shayna.

"It's the junior national championship," said Dan.

"And what if it's our only chance to find Minnie Maudde?" asked Shayna. "It's not like the adults have come up with a reasonable plan. Peanut brittle, joke bombs. Really. You know that will never help get Minnie Maudde back. It's crazy to think that would end the war."

"I suppose you are right," said Marie.

"You promise you won't say anything?" asked Dan.

"All right! I promeese."

Dan winked at Shayna. "Good. Let's go to the rafters tunnels."

"Now this is what I call fun," said Shayna.

CHAPTER TEN
The Rafters Tunnels

The three friends headed through the forest beyond the Gathering Stump. Dan led them to the Swinging Bridge to cross the Glass River.

Marie hesitated when they got to the bridge. "Oooh, I never take this bridge. Eet sways."

Dan gave a boring lecture on the engineering of the bridge. Marie yawned, poked Shayna with her elbow, and snorted. Shayna poked back, twice. The only thing they found important that Dan had to say about the bridge was, "So you see, even though the bridge doesn't look like it reaches the other side, it does because the whole bridge swings."

Marie raised her eyebrow. "That ees foolish. Why not build a bridge all the way across?"

"Where's the fun in that?" Shayna asked. "Come on, Marie. It'll be a blast."

Shayna was the first to step on the bridge and was closely followed by the others. The bridge started to swing back and forth like a thrilling amusement park ride. They grabbed the ropes, getting ever closer to the other side with each swing. The Swinging Bridge came to an abrupt stop when it reached the other side, and all three were tossed to the ground. Shayna skidded through a mud puddle on her derriere. The bridge creaked and moaned as though laughing.

"I get the feeling the bridge liked that," Shayna said, pulling her ponytail tight. Her jeans were now dirty, and her hair had collected strands of dry grass.

Shayna wiped herself off, and they ran to the rafters tunnels, stopping at the riverbank. They lingered at the riverbank, staring at the growing black crest of Caronstie that hung in the distant sky.

"I hate that thing," Shayna said.

"Yeah, me too," Marie said. "Okay, time to focus. Can I see your m.a.p.?"

Marie took the m.a.p. from Shayna, studied it closely, and scratched her head. She tapped her lips and closed her eyes. Just when it seemed she had nothing to say, she blurted, "Eet ees 'ard to tell where eet ees pointing because the tunnels are part of a 'uge mounce, but I think eet ees where there are four levels of tunnels and three branches off each."

"Wow," said Dan. "I don't know anyone else who would be able to figure that out. How do you know that?"

Marie shrugged and reexamined the map.

Dan sat down on the bank beside the watercourse and drew the interior of the tunnels for Shayna. Marie corrected him twice, to which Dan said, "I'm a finisher. I only ever need to go the fastest way through the tunnels."

To Shayna, the drawing looked like dozens of confused snakes intertwining and winding around one another.

"According to Jimmy Chow, there are fourteen main routes through the tunnel labyrinths," said Dan to Shayna.

"No, there are at least nineteen," said Marie.

"Quit correcting me!"

"Then get eet right, Mr. Smartypants. 'Ow can you not know I found more routes than Jimmy Chow?"

"Who's Jimmy Chow?" asked Shayna.

Marie was slow to answer. "'E was a first-star rafter. Played for Rafternoon T's. 'E always tried different routes during practices and sometimes would not find the way out of the tunnels for 'ours. But 'e learned the tunnels so well that 'e could almost always trick other rafters eento taking bad routes."

"Well?" Shayna asked. "What happened to him?"

Dan looked at the ground and dug the heel of his shoe into the sand. "Jimmy was practicing one night a few months ago. He wanted to test out a new route he found. He, uh … well, he went in the tunnel. We saw him go in. Marie and I both saw. The next morning when he hadn't yet come out of the tunnel, a search team was sent to find him. Samosby, from the Ministry, headed up the search team but never found Jimmy. He did a big report that concluded Jimmy must have drowned."

"We 'ad a funeral for 'im about a month ago," said Marie. "Eet was really sad. Eet was the first time I ever went to a funeral."

"Oh. I'm really sorry," said Shayna. She didn't know what else to say to her friends.

They all remained silent until Dan took a deep breath and said, "Let's do it. We're fine if we stick together. We have time before the tournament. Let's go in."

Dan gave Shayna a helmet and lifejacket at the top of the rafters launch. Shayna chose a cinnamon donut and picked at it to see how it tasted. Awesome, as expected.

Marie went down the launch first, followed by Shayna and then Dan. Marie handed out paddles that she plucked from a stack of paddles suspended overhead at the bottom of the launch.

"This is like a big water slide," said Shayna. Her voice echoed through the tunnels.

Some of the tunnels were steep and some had no slope at all. Shayna felt dizzy as they wound through miles of everglow rock. There were oodles of watery paths leading off the main tunnel, but Marie led them to a narrow section when she hung a left and disappeared down a waterfall.

Shayna stopped at the lip of the waterfall by dragging her paddle along the wall. Dan bumped her donut from behind and she plummeted over the falls.

"Ooooh. My stomach," said Shayna as she swirled in her donut at the bottom of the falls. "It's like a roller coaster but wet."

They floated through the meandering tunnel with Marie leading the way. The tunnel branched right, left, and also continued straight ahead. Marie turned on her helmet light as the everglow rock thinned.

"Let us take this branch to the right," Marie said. "No one ever goes this way. Eet ees so dark you 'ardly know eet ees 'ere." She marked their route with the chalk she always carried in her pocket.

The tunnels zigzagged and wound around each other, leaving Shayna with no idea where they had been or where they were headed. Water dripped from above and echoed through the tunnels.

Unevenly spaced along the stone walls were gargoyle figurines. Each had a different face, most of them with huge bulging eyeballs and sinister smirks. The tongues of some of the gargoyles dangled from their mouths as though tired of hanging on the wall.

"Waterfall! Hang on!" Dan yelled.

If it hadn't been for this warning, the drop in Shayna's stomach would have made her sick. She plummeted ten feet and then, within seconds, another forty feet.

Shayna came to rest at the bottom of the second falls, clinging to her donut. She swung her leg over the donut and struggled to pull herself on top. She looked like a drowned rat. It felt like her stomach was in her throat. Once aboard her donut, she found herself floating in a cavernous pond close to Dan.

Shayna heaved a huge sigh. "Wow! That was wicked." She paused and looked about her. "Uh, where are we?"

A thick mist floated above the water like fog in a cemetery on Halloween night.

"We're in Battler's Pond," Dan explained. "The main tributary tunnels converge in this pond. This is where finishers spar with stoppers to find the exit tunnel. It's hard to find it because of this darned mist, and even though I've gone through it hundreds of times, I still get lost."

She stood on her donut to see above the mist.

Battler's Pond sat at the bottom of a mammoth cave that stretched a hundred feet high. Waterfalls dropped from at least six different tunnels into the pond. There were long, pointed, icicle-shaped stalactites on the cavern ceiling that dripped water onto their heads. Five emblems adorned the dripping wet walls, one for each rafters team.

"Where's Marie?" asked Shayna. Shayna slipped off the donut and took a spectacular somersaulting plunge into the water, directly through the middle of her donut. "Oooph."

"I'm over 'ere," said Marie. Her voice echoed throughout the cave. She entered Battler's Pond, paddling from a different tunnel. "Why did you not follow me?"

"I thought we did," said Dan. "I thought you were right in front of us."

"There ees so leettle everglow rock een that section, I could barely see anything even with a 'elmet light," said Marie. "That ees a route I 'ave never taken before, for sure. I did not see any entrances that would go off een the direction of Caronstie. But there ees a spiral branch off the main path of level three, which ees much faster than taking the main path. Eet looks like the water flows upwards. Must be a strange optical illusion. Then there are four branches off that spiral. I can tell three of them go back towards Battler's Pond. But one branch I did not see at first. I went past eet because the water flows so fast. Eet ees really dark."

Dan stared at Marie, amazed by her ability to pick out the paths and store the information in her head. He boosted Shayna onto her donut with his foot.

"I know I could get some other teams lost eef I tricked them eento going een there. But I do not like eet at all. There was a 'uge creepy bat."

"No, you're seeing things, Marie," said Dan. "There aren't any bats in Terramanna. There aren't enough bugs for them to eat. There hasn't been a bat sighting in Terramanna in over four hundred and fifty-eight years."

"I am not seeing things, Mr. Know-Eet-All! And there *was* a bat sighting een Terramanna … two minutes ago, by me. Not four 'undred years ago."

"And fifty-eight," said Dan.

"Oh, shut up!" Marie said. She turned her donut and paddled through the fog to the exit tunnel.

"She's so sensitive," Dan said to Shayna. "And for the record, there are no bats in Terramanna."

CHAPTER ELEVEN
HISTORY LESSON

The three friends sat on the bank of the river. Dan apologized to Marie for acting like a know-it-all, and she admitted that it was possible that she could have been seeing things. Maybe she was just seeing shadows. After all, it was very dark.

"So, let's go back in tomorrow to see where the bat tunnel goes," said Shayna.

"Sheeze," said Dan. "There is no bat tunnel!"

"'E ees so sensitive," said Marie. *Snort.* "But, really, that tunnel ees the creepiest ever."

People started milling about the river banks. Scrumptions zipped toward the rafters area, some on hummingbirds, some on foot, and others using their own wings.

"We've gotta go," said Dan, looking at his watch. "We've got to get into our uniforms and warm-up."

"Good luck," shouted Shayna to her friends as they headed to the launch change rooms to join their team.

Shayna climbed the bleachers to level two and looked around for a seat—all donut-shaped, of course. A petite lady dressed in a blue suit held up a flashing sign: "Go Riff Rafts."

"Is this seat taken?" Shayna asked the chic lady.

"*Non, c'est pour vous.* Who are you cheering for?" asked the lady.

"The Riff Rafts," said Shayna. Everyone in the seats around them seemed to be wearing green and blue.

The lady tapped the donut beside her, and Shayna took a seat.

"Madam, are you French?" asked Shayna.

"You are very astute. French-Canadian. What gave it away?" asked the lady.

"Well, the French words for one thing," Shayna said with a grin.

The lady laughed and offered Shayna some of the steaming hot poutine that she carried in a bucket.

"This is my specialty. I came across the recipe in Quebec. Crispy golden fries and fresh cheese curds smothered in creamy velouté gravy, a dash of ground black pepper, and a pinch of Atlantic seasoning salt." The lady made the poutine sound very glamorous. "It certainly isn't the way to keep trim, but it is delicious nonetheless. Go ahead; try some."

The woman had shiny, short, ebony hair that flattered her heart-shaped face. She had emerald eyes and fine features. Her lips were full.

Aha! Shayna knew who looked just like her. "Hey, you're Marie's mom!"

"Yes, I am," said the woman. "Ah, you must be Marie's new friend."

Shayna nodded and smiled, quite happy that Marie shared news of their blossoming friendship with her mother. Shayna noticed that the lady did not have any accent.

"Call me Annette," said Marie's mother. "You know, my daughter is very fond of you."

"I really like Marie. She's so smart. Definitely best friend material. Oh, and her mother makes great poutine," quipped Shayna, helping herself to more of Annette's delicious concoction.

All of the rafters teams made their way onto the field, each donning bright uniforms, except the GiRafts, who wore dull brown and puce jerseys. The teams were introduced over the loudspeakers by a Gomock commentator. When the Riff Rafts were announced, Annette whistled so loudly that Shayna instantly gained respect for her.

The teams assembled at the top of the launch. The sneaks burst into action down the launch when the gong sounded. The five stoppers followed. Each snatched a sugar cane paddle at the overhead paddle grab and sped toward the tunnel. The Riff Rafts cheering section roared as Marie disappeared into the tunnel a hair before the others. Atlas and the other two Skytrak coaches did somersaults in the air.

With the next reverberating gong, three blockers per team launched. Four fumbled at the paddle grab, and so they were up the river without a paddle until their recoverers launched thirty seconds later.

When the final gong sounded, the finishers from each team, including Dan, rocketed off the top of the launch and into the tunnel.

Referees wearing orange blazers and headsets ducked into the tunnel, blowing whistles and making wild hand signals.

The Gomock commentator, announcing from a balloon equipped with scads of television cameras, speculated as to what might be happening in the tunnels. The commentator introduced the players on every team as their photos, helmet size, and favorite ice cream flavors appeared on the screens. When he reached Dan's name, he said, "Dan Bailey, finisher for the Riff Rafts. I hope he knows what he's in for up against Rafteralls' new stopper, Janic Ismanov, because he's one guy you wouldn't want to meet in a dark tunnel. I'm not filled with confidence that Bailey will even find his way to Battler's Pond."

The Riff Rafts cheering section booed at the announcer. The announcer booed back.

Two rows in front of Shayna, a girl turned around and smirked. Ugh! Christie.

Christie shouted, "Hey, now I know why it stinks here. Prophecy Girl's right behind us."

"Stuff a sock in it, blondie," growled Shayna. "The only thing that reeks is your personality."

Annette snorted a laugh. Shayna knew she had really gotten Christie's goat because Christie got up and left with her nose pointed high in the air and her entourage in tow.

As Christie waddled away in her miniskirt, Shayna couldn't help but notice the crest of Caronstie lingering in the sky in the distance. Shayna's stomach knotted with the thought of being stranded. Minnie Maudde was her only hope to ever go home.

"So, Annette," Shayna said, "do you know Minnie Maudde?"

"Minnie Maudde?" asked Annette. "Oh, yes. Yes, I know her well. Why?"

"Oh, I was just curious."

"I see," said Annette. She swallowed a fry. "So, I understand that you are Shayna of the Prophecy."

Heads turned to look at Shayna. She felt embarrassed.

Annette continued in a whisper. "And, if indeed you are that person, I know you can't sit still with the thought of our chief scientist being compromised."

"Exactly," said Shayna. "But the Balloon Lady doesn't even want me to think about it. I need to get Minnie Maudde back to Terramanna. But the Balloon Lady just keeps telling me to have fun, fun, fun. She won't tell me anything."

"Well, there is good reason for that. The constitution is very clear about fun," said Annette. "But I think you're on the right track. I agree that Terramanna must take immediate steps to save Minnie Maudde. She's our chief scientist. She creates things. The very things that make Terramanna fun. Take, for instance, the zero calorie organic chocolate chip cookie dough milkshake, my favorite. Or the sweet green butter churned from avocados. Or jumping jelly beans. Floating pancakes. Musical mist balls. Tree stairwells. She knows chemical reactions and properties of physics that you and I could never even dream of. She leads a brilliant scientific team, and discoveries like hers are the primary reason Terramanna is so much fun today. And Falco wants to destroy all that fun."

"Why?" Shayna asked.

"It's all about history," Annette answered. "Centuries ago, the Terramans discovered that everglow rock is a clean energy source and regenerates itself. The Caronsties saw the technological advancements we made as a result of the unlimited power derived from this rock, and they wanted to cash in on it.

"The Caronsties learned that our source of everglow rock came from beneath Lake Orange. So, they bored to the source and mined it for years without Terramanna's knowledge. They sold everglow rock to other countries and made a lot of money, which Falco used to fortify the barriers."

A Skytrak fluttered up the stairs, shouting, "Binovision glasses. Get your free binovision flavor arm glasses here. Special price today only."

Annette raised her hand. "Two please."

The Skytrak handed over two sets of eyeglasses.

Shayna put on her over-sized binovision glasses and could see the finish line up close. Even more fun, the arm of the glasses was a high-tech straw that transmitted flavor images to Shayna's mouth.

"Oooh. They're like binoculars only they're glasses. Awesome!" Shayna fiddled with the focus on her glasses, sucked on the flavor arm, and then asked, "So, what happened after the Caronsties stole the everglow rock?"

"Terramanna expanded its territory to the east and, as a result, power needs increased," said Annette. "When Terramanna sought to tap into more of the rock, it was discovered that a lot of it was gone. Terramanna found a huge mine beneath Lake Orange that the Caronsties had created. A war erupted over their actions."

Shayna blinked a few times and then a light bulb went off in her head. She asked, "Is that mine beneath Lake Orange now called Hypogeal Park?"

"You are truly quite bright, aren't you?" said Annette. "Eventually the Terramans were able to push the Caronsties back to their own land and away from the mines, but a lot of lives were lost. The Terramans threatened that they would take steps to get the everglow rock back and return it to its home under the lake. It is partly because of these threats that the Caronsties built barriers encircling their lands, barriers that no one has ever survived ... horrid barriers at every possible entrance to Caronstie. They permitted only one sliver of airspace for our use, which as you know is now closed to our balloons."

Shayna took a long sip from her flavor arm, which was now transmitting a combination of sour lemon and sweet grape flavors.

Annette carried on, "Anyway the power in the stolen rock gradually died. We could see Caronstie's lights fade as the rock's power diminished over time. Our rock remains fully charged because we have never moved it from its original location, which is the only place it thrives eternally.

"Now that the stolen rock has died, we believe that the Caronsties are planning to invade to get more. But we know that this time they intend to be smarter about it. They learned that they can't move the everglow rock and keep it eternally active, so they plan to get rid of us instead so that they can use the rock in its current location for their own power needs.

"The only problem Monsieur Falco has with this plan is that Terramanna is so much fun. You see, before the barriers were built, Caronstie lost a large group of its warriors when they defected from Caronstie to live a fabulously fun life right here in Terramanna. That is another reason that the barriers were built: to keep anyone from leaving Caronstie. We know that Falco is worried it could happen again. He would never accept a further defection of citizens.

"Yes, as you can see, Falco's plan is undoubtedly to destroy Terramanna."

"I can't let that happen," said Shayna. She surprised herself by feeling suddenly protective of Terramanna. "And, why shouldn't people have fun?"

"Indeed." Annette smiled.

"Where is the barrier in the mine?"

"Hmm, I never really thought about it. But I suppose there must be one," replied Annette.

Shayna and Annette were shocked back into the present by the blaring voice of the Gomock commentator. "We have word from the reporting referee that the stoppers for the Pack Rafts, Rafteralls, and Riff Rafts have all made their way into Battler's Pond."

Shayna cheered, but her mind was elsewhere. She pulled her m.a.p. out of her pocket. "Mr. Map, where is the barrier in Hypogeal Park?"

The map displayed "Searching Archives" and then hummed and whirred as though on a secret mission.

The applauding was now overwhelming. And to make the event even more uproarious, everyone wearing binovision flavor arm glasses was experiencing an explosion of flavors. Shayna could hardly contain her enthusiasm because it tasted so great. She sucked on the arm of her binovision glasses and wiggled her rear end, dancing on her seat … until she fell off, landing on her posterior in the poutine.

The Gomock voice thundered, "All stoppers are straggling in now. The blockers have been unable to block both the Rafteralls and Pack Rafts finishers. Both are now in the Pond, sparring with stoppers. Ah, I have just received an updated report. All finishers but the Riff Rafts' are now in Battler's Pond. I'm getting reports that David Johns, the Riff Rafts stopper, is sparring with all of them. Surprisingly fantastic plays he's making! A referee is transmitting a signal. Ah, finally Dan Bailey has entered the Pond."

More rooting! More cheering! More uncontrollable dancing! The crowd was going wild.

"This is going to be a fight to the end, folks. But I give the advantage to the Rafteralls. Johns can't fend them off forever!"

With this comment, the Rift Rafts fans blew raspberries at the Gomock commentator. The Gomock blew loud, wet raspberries back.

The Balloon Lady paraded around in a tie-dyed bathing suit, royal-blue-sequined harem pants, and a matching bathing cap adorned with a single ostrich feather. She stood at the top of the rafters launch, clutching a box that changed colors with each update from the commentator.

Two finishers broke through the end of the tunnel and paddled like demons through the snaky waters.

"That's Dan!" Shayna sprung to her feet and chanted, "Bai-ley! Bai-ley! Bai-ley!" Fans joined Shayna, and the noise level rose to an earth-shaking roar.

Shayna danced as she chanted. She convinced other fans near her to wiggle their posteriors and dance too. However, no one else had gravy on their derriere like Shayna.

People in two sections of the bleachers were howling, "Pack Rafts pack a punch! Pack Rafts pack a punch!" But the "Bai-ley" sections overpowered them.

Players from other teams exploded from the exit, paddling like maniacs. Rafters protected their finishers from harm as they hustled through treacherous chutes.

Dan forced the Pack Rafts finisher into the riverbank. Dan plummeted over the falls, breaking the tape at the finish line. Candy fireworks exploded.

The fans' exuberance oozed into every pore of Shayna's body. She jumped up and down, hugging everyone near her. So many scrumptions sneezed throughout the bleachers that it seemed like a cloudburst.

The Balloon Lady opened the box and released hundreds of green and blue mini balloons into the air. They floated away in all directions like a flock of doves, and exploded miles away, spewing candy far and wide.

In the distance, the Popcorn Volcano erupted, spurting plump popcorn high into the sky. Butter lava flowed down the side of the volcano. The scent of hot buttered popcorn filled the air.

Shayna couldn't remember ever having more fun.

CHAPTER TWELVE
CHAMPIONS

Sugar Beach was packed with fans wielding cameras. Dan wrapped up an interview with a Ploomi sports reporter. The rest of the Riff Rafts whooped it up in the sand. Elated scrumptions poured wheelbarrows full of blue and green candied sand on the beach. Shayna raced to Marie and gave her an energetic high-five.

"That was so much fun. I could barely stand it!" said Shayna. "Your team is fantastic."

Marie pulled Shayna aside to a quiet spot on the beach where they perched on the edge of a sand dune. "I saw another bat. I went back eento that creepy tunnel because Dan convinced me I was just seeing things. I thought eet would be great to trick some other rafters eento taking that route. But then I saw a 'uge bat. Eet ees really freaky to 'ave a bat coming right at you een a narrow tunnel." Marie shuddered.

"Hey," said Dan. "Are you two hiding over here?" He seemed to appear out of nowhere.

Under her breath, Marie said, "Do not tell Mr. Know-Eet-All. I cannot take another lecture."

"Congratulations, Dan!" said Shayna. "You were amazing."

"Thanks," said Dan. He winked at Shayna. "Let's go. The awards ceremony is going to start soon at Scrumption Stadium. The queens are giving out the trophies!"

The trio hurried toward Scrumption Stadium, through the throng of fans. Shayna's gravy covered rear-end was now quite a spectacle because blue and green candy sprinkles were smushed into the gravy.

"Marie, I have a confession," said Dan while waving at his adoring fans. He continued with a soft voice so no one in the crowd could hear. "I think you might have been right about the bat."

"Continue," said Marie.

"The reason I was last into Battler's Pond was because I found Lars Shermann from the GiRafts screaming in a tunnel branching from the level three spiral tunnel. Lars said he had seen monster bats and was too petrified to move. I convinced Lars that there were no bats in Terramanna and helped him make his way back to the main tunnel. I couldn't just leave him there."

"Apology accepted," said Marie. She slapped Dan on the back.

Ding!

"Oh, I almost forgot," said Shayna. She pulled the m.a.p. from her pocket. "I knew it!"

"What ees eet?"

"We can get into Caronstie through the barrier in Hypogeal Park."

"What barrier?" asked Dan.

"The jungle behind the diamond glass wall."

"But your m.a.p. did not say anything about going through the jungle. Eet said to get een through the tunnels," said Marie.

"Oh, I get it," said Dan. "The m.a.p. database doesn't know about the hole in the glass. M.a.p.s don't detect information properly underground near everglow rock. Subsurface features have to be entered manually."

"Are you thinking that there are two ways eento Caronstie? 'Ypogeal Park and the tunnels?" asked Marie.

"Yeah," said Shayna. "I was in Caronstie and I didn't even know it!"

"But that can't be," said Dan. "No one has ever survived a barrier … not even my parents."

"Listen, it makes sense," said Shayna. "I sat with Marie's mom during the tournament. She told me that there is a barrier at every entrance to Caronstie. She also said the Caronsties dug under Terramanna and made the mines that are now Hypogeal Park."

"Mines?" asked Marie.

"I think she's talking about the mines created by the Caronsties hundreds of years ago to steal Terramanna's everglow rock," said Dan. "Obediah Nightshade was the scrumption that discovered the mines and theft of the everglow rock. He was a descendant of—"

"Enough already, Mr. Know-Eet-All," said Marie. "Carry on, Shayna."

"After talking to your mom, I asked my m.a.p. where the barrier is in Hypogeal Park. Look what it says," said Shayna, passing the m.a.p. to Marie.

"Jungle," read Marie. "So, that glass wall ees just there to keep us safe from the jungle barrier?"

"I guess Terramanna made the best of the mines and created a park out of it," said Shayna. "This is great. Now we don't have to find the entrance through the tunnels. That could take forever. We already know we can get in through the jungle barrier."

"I'm not going through a barrier," said Dan. "That's how my parents died."

"I agree. Eet ees way too dangerous," said Marie.

"Well, I've survived the jungle barrier once. I can do it again," said Shayna.

"Are you really that stupid? Or just conceited?" blurted Dan. His face turned red. "Why would you think you can get through a barrier when my parents couldn't even do it? How dare you think you're better than them!"

Dan ran into the crowd, leaving Marie and Shayna standing in the midst of the cheering and singing revelers.

"What did I do?" asked Shayna.

"I think you scared 'im. 'E knows 'ow dangerous eet ees. You know, because of 'is parents. Dan ees the only orphan een our school."

Shayna felt awful. She knew exactly what it felt like to be an orphan. But at least she had her grandfather ... if only she could get back home to him. Her heart felt like it was sinking.

"One way or another, I'm going to get to Caronstie," said Shayna. "I've got to find Minnie Maudde."

"I know. But I am sorry. I cannot go with you. Eet ees no fun at all een a barrier. I do not want to let you down because you are my friend. But I cannot go."

"I guess I'm on my own then." Shayna swallowed hard. She clutched her m.a.p. to her chest. "I'm going through the jungle. I know I can."

"What about the tunnel entrance?" asked Marie. "Eet might be safer."

"We still don't know exactly where the entrance is in the tunnels, right?"

Marie nodded.

"So it could take a long time to find it, right?"

"Uh huh," said Marie.

"And Jimmy Chow got lost in there even though he knew his way around the tunnels."

"True," said Marie.

"And the bats fly at you in those skinny tunnels. I really hate bats," said Shayna. The thought of it made her skin crawl. She tossed her ponytail off her shoulder.

The crowd around them grew denser and louder as they approached Scrumption Stadium. Fans scooped up Marie and carried her on their shoulders into the stadium, leaving Shayna standing alone in the mass of people.

"Hey, Prophecy Girl!" shouted someone from the crowd. "Your dirty pants make me wanna gag."

It was Christie. Yuck! Shayna knew she couldn't take any more of that prima donna's comments. So, she turned around and headed against the crowd.

She flagged down a balloon taxi to catch a ride to the Sweet Suites. As the yellow and black checkered balloon rose in the air, Shayna noticed two women dressed in fancy velvet gowns perched on a giant newt-drawn chariot. The candied jewels in their tiaras sparkled. The twin queens! The chariot followed a red carpet that led all the way into the stadium. Shayna leaned over the basket to watch the royal pair, and her binovision glasses fell from her head and plunked to the floor of the chariot in front of the queens. The contingent of royal guards whipped out their muck handguns and sprayed cotton candy floss into the crowd.

Christie wound up entangled in the sticky floss, screaming.

"Oops! Sorry," said Shayna from the balloon taxi as it transported her away, high above the crowd. She chuckled. "Now that was fun."

Shayna arrived at her condo to find an elfin dinner balloon waiting for her with a covered plate inside the basket. Shayna took the plate out of the basket and the balloon zipped away.

She lifted the shiny cover off the rock sugar plate to find a small green disc and a note. She read the note aloud. "Add three drops of water to the disc. Enjoy your meal."

Shayna followed the instructions. With the third drop, the disc exploded into a sinfully delicious dinner of cheese soufflé, square pellets that turned into strawberry slices on the tongue, broccoli that grew into fist-sized vegetable trees before her eyes, a mug of milk, and a marble-sized yellow and blue striped ball stamped with the words "musical mist ball."

Shayna sat at the desk and savored the ambrosial meal. The musical mist ball disintegrated on her tongue. Every time she opened her mouth, flavored mist escaped, belting Beethoven's "Ode to Joy."

"This is brilliant."

On the last note from the musical mist ball, Shayna stared out the wall of windows at the crest of Caronstie that hovered over the castle in the distance. Her mind swirled with thoughts of Minnie Maudde.

"Tomorrow, Minnie Maudde. I'm coming for you tomorrow."

CHAPTER THIRTEEN
BEST FRIENDS

Dan was feeling as though he had let down Shayna. At the celebration of champions, he was so upset that he actually agreed to meet Christie for lunch. Dan convinced himself that this was not a date and ignored the fact that Christie would think otherwise.

"Anyway, she's a fraud," said Christie as she sipped grape juice from a sugar crystal goblet at Muldoon's World Eatery. She twirled her flirty blonde hair around her index finger. "She's so normal in every sense of the word."

Dan started to fume. Shayna might be conceited enough to think she could get through a barrier but she was at least trying to do something good.

"I wish you'd quit talking about her like that," said Dan. "Shayna's got a kind heart and she's very brave."

"Oh, get real," said Christie. She flipped open a compact and smeared pink lip gloss on her pouty lips. "She is not brave, just stupid. She's sloppy and not pretty at all. And she's warped enough to think she's Terramanna's savior." Christie snapped shut the compact. "We'd all be better off without her."

"What do you know about Shayna? All you do is torment her. You haven't spent one minute getting to know her." Dan was trying not to yell in this fancy diner but couldn't help it. "She doesn't even know if she's *the* Shayna. I'm sure she'd rather not be."

"There's no need to defend her, Dan. That is, unless you've got something going with her. Is that it? You like her?" Christie's eyes widened. "How dare you! How dare you prefer that stuck-up urchin over me!"

"Stuck-up? Look in the mirror!"

"I hate you, Dan. I hate your pretty-boy hair. I hate your eyes. I hate everything about you. You deserve to be an orphan!"

Dan glared at Christie. This non-date was now over. He flew out of his seat and sprinted from the restaurant all the way home.

He burst through his condo door.

"Sandy! Sandy! Are you home?"

Sandy dashed from the kitchen. He had whipped cream in his hair, and butter tart filling spilled down the front of his apron. Flour plastered his right ear and cheek.

"Why do I have to be an orphan? What did I do to deserve this?" Dan wiped his eyes with the palms of his hands.

Sandy grew to Dan's height and wiped flour from his bushy brow with his apron. "You don't deserve to be an orphan. You deserve only the best. You know, your parents loved you very much." He patted Dan on the shoulder. "Sit. It's time we talk."

Dan curled up in the fluffiest white chair in the living room and sniffled. He hated being an orphan. He hated that he couldn't even remember his parents. Why would they have gone anywhere near that stupid scorpion breeding ground? Why did they do that to him?

"First," said Sandy, "let's taste some of my epicurean creations."

Sandy clapped his hands twice and the lights went off. "Oops." Another clap turned the lights back on.

He clapped his hands three times and a cart piled high with warm butter tarts, fruit turnovers, and personal pies rolled out of the kitchen into the living room.

Sandy took a butter tart and threw his apron over the handle of the cart. A cloud of flour wafted from the apron.

Dan stared at him. "Well?"

"Righto, let's get started," said Sandy. He pulled a chair in front of Dan and handed him a soursop turnover. "There are some things I never told you about your parents. The timing was bad in that, until now, you've been too young. But … I guess there's no time like the present." Sandy cleared his throat. "Your parents and I were the best of friends."

"I know," said Dan. "You've told me that before."

"Don't get snippy," said Sandy. "This is not easy for me to talk about."

"Sorry."

"As I was saying, your parents and I were best of friends. We were also excellent friends with another couple, Sarah and Alex. We were all very intent on helping the Caronsties experience the fun, frivolity, and merriment that we freely enjoy in Terramanna. It just seems so wrong that we all have wildly fantastic existences, yet the Caronsties endure lives of destitution, sadness, and fear. Alas, we recognized the need to get into Caronstie to be able to help.

"So, we studied the barriers day and night for two and a half years. We had to find a way in. We had this crazy schmazy idea that if we could find a safe way, we could send a team in to teach the Caronsties how to create for themselves the things we love so much about Terramanna.

"Anyway, we eventually recognized that a distant part of the rafters tunnels lays above a relatively unknown barrier. No one really knows anything about this barrier, a subterranean jungle."

"You mean the one in the old mines?" asked Dan.

"Yes," said Sandy, shocked that Dan knew anything about this barrier. He took a bite of his maple butter tart. It dripped down his chin. "Anyhoo, Sarah had located the tunnel using quite a complex mounce variable calculation she found in an ancient scrumption calculus text. She was quite a math whiz. Won several awards, you know. So, Alex went with Sarah to explore the tunnels, just to see if her calculations were correct and whether they would lead into the subterranean jungle from the tunnels above. They pick-axed their way through some stone into a cavern, and Sarah fell through the crumbling floor. Alex tried to grab her, but she fell out of his grip into the net of vines in the jungle below."

"Did Sarah die?"

"Not right away. Alex could hear her. Anyway, a slew of enormous bats raced up toward the hole just as Alex yelled out to her that he would come to get her. Alex had no choice but to cover over the hole to keep from getting swarmed by thousands of bats."

"He just left her there? He didn't even try to get her?" asked Dan, stunned.

"Don't be ridiculous," said Sandy. He helped himself to a steaming pomegranate personal pie. "Alex raced back through the tunnels to get your parents and me. We told the queens what had happened, but they were taking so long to get a rescue team together that we couldn't wait any longer. Bureaucracy was holding everything up. You know how it is with governments. Lots of red tape. In this case, extremely sticky red tape. So, we took the rescue into our own hands."

"What did you do?" asked Dan. He sat on the edge of the chair.

"Our barrier research convinced us that the scorpion breeding ground was the safest accessible route into Caronstie. The plan was for Alex and your parents to cross the breeding ground while I was to stay back and distract the eagles. There weren't so many eagles back then. Anyway, your parents and Alex were wearing a new invention to protect themselves from the scorpions: liquid armor. Once in Caronstie, they were going to access the jungle from the Caronstie side. We figured that if they didn't shake up the tree canopy, they wouldn't have to worry about the bats.

"But the plan failed." Sandy sobbed. "The liquid armor disintegrated at the edge of the scorpion breeding ground in the acid mist that rose up from Cackle Creek.

"We didn't know that liquid armor wouldn't work near acid. I should have checked with Minnie Maudde, but we were in such a hurry. It was so stupid of me not to think of the acid." Sandy held a pillow to his face and wept.

Dan didn't know what to think or say. His mind was swirling with images of his parents.

"I'm so sorry, Dan." Sandy blew his nose on his napkin. "They almost made it."

"They were trying to save someone." Dan sniffled and wiped his eyes. He smiled and expelled a long breath. "My parents were trying to save someone."

Sandy nodded. "They had incredibly kind hearts. They were very brave."

"Thanks, Sandy. For everything." For the first time in his life, Dan was proud to be an orphan, proud his parents were courageous and risked their own lives to try to save their friend.

The moment was interrupted by the sudden blaring of pop music originating from the doorbell. The upbeat doorbell always lifted spirits.

"Wahoo! That must be the Balloon Lady," said Sandy as he bolted upright and leaped about the room to the music like a disabled gazelle.

"You are truly a hideous dancer, you know," said Dan. He could never contain his laughter when Sandy put on his groove. That was just one of the things he loved about Sandy.

"Right here in this very room I am having a dignitary meeting to discuss the latest developments in the war," said Sandy. He belly danced toward a button on the wall and pressed it with his hip.

The Balloon Lady pranced into the room with her magenta and red taffeta gown billowing about her. A brilliant headdress of newly shed oriole and magpie feathers adorned her head.

"Good day," said the Balloon Lady. "I see the others have yet to arrive." She pulled a set of opera glasses from her blue zebra-striped purse and examined the pastry cart. Sandy's belly dancing didn't seem to distract her in the least. "I realize that I may be running a smidgen early but will certainly make an exit and reappearance in two shakes of a lamb's tail if that is your wish." She helped herself to a peach pineapple personal pie.

"Wish schmish. Of course not," said Sandy. "You're always welcome. Dan and I were just discussing Sarah and Alex."

"Excellent!" said the Balloon Lady. "So now you know about Shayna's parents. It's been so exhausting for me to keep that bottled up inside for so long."

"Huh?" said Dan. He looked like he had just been run over by a tractor. "Alex and Sarah were Shayna's parents?"

Sandy held his temples and shook his head.

"Ooops," said the Balloon Lady. She bit her bottom lip. The feathers of her headdress sagged.

"Her parents and my parents …"

"Trampled tomatoes! I shouldn't have said anything." The Balloon Lady clasped her hand over her mouth.

"I have to go," said Dan. He hugged Sandy as though he might never get another chance and ran out the door.

CHAPTER FOURTEEN

BARRIER BOUND

"M.a.p., where is Shayna?"

Ding! Dan viewed his m.a.p., which showed Shayna's location in the shopping district, on Cake Walk. She was with Marie. Had it been any other girls, he would have thought they were simply shopping for shoes. But he knew that Shayna and Marie weren't thinking about shoes. He had no doubt that Marie was taking Shayna to Hinklehand's Hoard, a store with more gadgets than anyone could use in an entire lifetime. These were the type of gadgets perfect for an attempted rescue of Minnie Maudde.

He caught a balloon taxi and landed at the doors to Hinklehand's Hoard. The store was packed with people stocking up on items because of the war. Rafters fans stared at Dan as he made his way through the throng of patrons. He hardly noticed the attention.

He found the girls on level five.

"I think you should take a muck gun," said Marie to Shayna.

"No guns," said Shayna. "I don't want anyone getting hurt. Plus, don't you need some kind of a permit for that?"

Dan appeared from behind a shelf and interrupted. "Actually, you have to be sixteen and pass a training course. Six people were seriously hurt by muck gun fire before they brought in the muck training laws twenty-eight years ago. Since then, not one single injury."

The girls were shocked to see Dan.

"Dan?" said Shayna. "How did you find … aren't you mad at …"

"We should make a list of the things we'll need to take with us," Dan said.

"We?" said Shayna.

"Yep. I'm going with you." Dan pulled out his m.a.p. and dictated a list as he walked down the aisles with the girls chasing behind. "We'll need four rolls of stretch gum, two bags of meal discs—we can leave there what we don't eat—gumplosion balls of various sizes, musical mist balls, goo grenades, voice-activated matches, a couple bags of sugar cement, a sac of tracking beads …"

Shayna put her hand to his lips. "You're going with me?"

"Yeah. Is that a problem?"

"I thought you were mad at me," said Shayna. "You told me I was stupid and conceited to think I could do this."

"Trying to save someone is the most honorable thing anyone could do. Besides, how could you have any fun doing this without me?" Dan scanned the gadgets on the shelves as he walked.

Marie snorted. "Yeah. Your lectures are a laugh a minute." *Snort.*

"And we need you," Dan said as he pointed at Marie, "Terramanna's champion sneak, to sidetrack people while we make our way through Hypogeal Park into the jungle."

"I could 'ave fun doing that," said Marie.

When they left Hinklehand's Hoard, Dan and Shayna had so much survival gear that they would have needed a station wagon to transport it all were it not for their bottomless pit pockets.

By the time they were at the Hypogeal Park entrance, they had devised their plan of action. Dan summarized the plan. "When we get near the Jungle Ryde Tour sign, Marie will distract people by offering her autograph. Shayna and I will go into the jungle through the smashed glass wall and wait for Boobie."

"Okay. And, like eet or not, eef you are not back een five hours, I am telling the Balloon Lady where you are."

"All right," said Dan. "Don't be such a worry wart."

Marie was silent. Scared.

"Marie, we'll be fine," said Shayna. "We'll be with Boobie. I think he's in the jungle all the time. Once we're through the jungle, it's a cinch."

Dan twisted the fireworks doorknob against the wall, and the door to Hypogeal Park swung open.

"Shayna's Fun Force has entered the building," joked Dan.

Marie snorted.

"Fun force," said Shayna as they descended in the elevator. "I like it. It has a certain ring to it."

The friends made their way through the crowds in Hypogeal Park. Rafters fans slapped Dan and Marie on their backs and cheered as they passed.

As planned, Marie gave out autographs near the Jungle Ryde Tour sign, and a long line of autograph seekers formed in front of her. When she next looked back, Shayna and Dan were gone.

A lump formed in her throat, terrified that this would be the last time she would ever see her friends.

CHAPTER FIFTEEN
BOOBIE SCHUMPERT

Dan and Shayna slipped through the hole in the glass wall. Within seconds, the rickety bus skidded to a stop on the path alongside Shayna and Dan. The bus doors creaked open, and Boobie Schumpert stood in the open doorway, his hands on his hips. A flake of skin fluttered from his neck to the ground.

"Me friend. I'm so glad yer back," Boobie said. "I missed ya."

"Hi, Mr. Schumpert. It's nice to see you again," said Shayna. "This is my friend, Dan."

"Nice to meet you, sir," said Dan. Dan stuck out his hand to shake Boobie's, but Boobie didn't know what to make of the gesture or what to think of being called sir. Yet he knew he now had another friend.

"We brought you something," said Shayna. She reached into her bottomless pit pocket, pulled out a small gift-wrapped box, and handed it to him. "I hope you like it."

"Oh," said Boobie. "It's really perty. What d'ya calls it?"

"It's a gift," said Dan.

"A gift? I never saw no gift before. It's beautiful." A tear trickled down Boobie's cheek.

"You've never seen a present?" asked Shayna.

"No," said Boobie. "And I ain't never seen a gift neither."

Shayna and Dan looked at one another.

"Astounding," said Dan.

"Mr. Schumpert, a gift is something someone gives to another person to show they like him," said Shayna. "Open it. You'll see. It's fun."

Boobie inspected the present. "Where's it open up?"

"Tear the paper off," said Shayna.

Boobie looked horrified.

"The gift is on the inside," said Dan.

Excitement exploded from Boobie like a kid on Christmas morning. He peeled back the ribbon and paper, making sure not to rip any of it. He pulled a burgundy wallet out of the wrapping. He was puzzled.

"What is it?" asked Boobie, opening and closing the flap of the wallet.

"It's a mounce wallet to put all your money in," said Dan. "It's from Hinklehand's Hoard."

"I ain't got no money," said Boobie.

"Well, you can put almost anything in it," said Shayna. "Watch this." She took the wallet from him and put everything she could find in it, including the bucket of fiberglass resin from under his seat.

Boobie squealed. Torrents of joy gushed from every pore of his body. It was like he had won the lottery. He ran from the bus and laughed hysterically as he stuffed fruit and nuts from the jungle floor into the wallet.

Out of the blue, Boobie dropped to his knees and sobbed.

"What's wrong, Mr. Schumpert?" asked Dan.

"I don't want ya gettin' hurt bein' here," said Boobie. "You two should get back to Terramanna. This jungle ain't a safe place to be."

"Then why are you here?" asked Shayna.

"Me friends, I bin sorta outcast from Caronstie since I was born. It's me name does it to me."

Boobie sniffled like a lost child. Dan and Shayna looked at each other, not knowing what to do.

"Go on, Boobie," said Shayna. "Let it all out. You'll feel better." She patted him on the back.

So let it out he did. "You see, when I was born and me name was announced, everyone laughed. T'was the first laughter that had been heard publicly in years. Me parents refused to change me name when Falco demanded. They felt it was a good name … a cheerful name. So, Falco hung me parents for disobedience and promoting community cheer. Then he ordered me to a life in the dungeons, serving prisoners."

"Oh, I'm so sorry to hear about your parents," said Shayna. She sat cross-legged next to him on the jungle floor. "My parents died too. A long time ago."

"Mine also … in the scorpion breeding ground," said Dan.

"Both yers too?" Boobie wiped his nose on the back of his hand. "We all have so much in common, ain't we?"

Shayna nodded. "But why are you in the jungle?"

"As I were sayin', I lived in the dungeons all me life. Then, just a few years ago, Falco offered me the chance to be free. He said if I found a way to get through the jungle, he'd let me change me name and live a normal life. Well, it took a whole two years to learn me way around the jungle. Almost got meself killed many a times. Every day I would leave those terrible dungeons and go deeper into the jungle. At night I went back to the dungeons or stayed in one of them blue-barred stingin' beetle shelters that I built.

"Finally, two months ago I made me way through the entire jungle after I cleared the last of the old mining routes. 'Bout a month ago Falco made me drive him to the diamond glass wall. On his orders, his dumb ministers tore a hole through the diamond glass into Terramanna with a newfangled laser blaster. One minister lost his left arm it got so burnt up using the laser.

Never seen such a machine. Fancy as the laser was, it still took two whole days to get through the glass, it did.

"Falco and his men took off to Terramanna through the hole in the glass and came back haulin' a woman. She was gagged and tied."

"What happened to the woman?" Shayna blurted. She could hardly keep from exploding with glee. She knew Boobie must be talking about Minnie Maudde.

"I drove the lady and Falco back to the dungeons. The old bird left some of his ministers in the jungle to find their own way home. They never made it back. The hinks took care of 'em. I knew Falco was a vile piece o' work, but leaving his own loyal men in the jungle is too much. He makes me sick. He's such a … such a chicken."

Boobie wiped his nose with a rag and put it in his wallet. He continued, "I figured that I had met me end of the bargain and should get a new, boring name. But Falco said I had to get him some Terramans for head loppin' in the public square. I was supposed to get him ten o' yer kind, all kids, and then he promised to set me free with a whole new name. So, I set up the Jungle Ryde Tour to get young 'uns to take to Falco. I put up some signs, but no one ever came—'cept you, that is."

Shayna gulped. She realized that Boobie could have been more dangerous than anything else in that jungle.

Boobie continued, "But I couldn't turn ya in. Yer me friend. After ya was gone, I remembered in me heart how scared ya was. I can't do that to no kids."

Boobie wiped his eyes again. "Now I ain't never gonna get me new name."

"Falco cheated you," said Dan. "You know, if you lived in Terramanna, your name would be honored. The funnier the name, the better. Terramanna is about fun, frivolity, and merriment."

"Fun? That's nonsense. I can't have no fun," Boobie blubbered.

"No, it's not nonsense," said Shayna. "In fact, the lady that Falco took prisoner, Minnie Maudde, she has all kinds of fun up her sleeves."

"Right up her sleeves?" asked Boobie. He stopped weeping, pulled the old rag out of the wallet, and dabbed his wet eyes.

"If you knew her, you'd see how much fun she creates," said Dan. "She's the chief scientist. We're here to rescue her and take her back to Caronstie."

"Well, ya ain't got much time. Falco is gonna kill her tonight."

"No!" cried Shayna. Her throat welled with a lump.

"D'ya wants the kid? He's due for his execution too."

"What kid?" Dan asked.

"The one that dropped out of the sky a few months back. Right near the waterfall he plopped. The kid had lots o' sweets with him and was wearin' a funny helmet. Must be one o' yers," replied Boobie.

"Jimmy! Falco has Jimmy too!" Dan fell to his knees. "Oh, please, Mr. Schumpert. Help us rescue Jimmy. I will be forever grateful to you if you help us rescue Jimmy too."

"He don't deserve no harm," said Boobie with a shrug.

Monkeys of various kinds sneaked up to Dan and snatched meal discs from his pockets.

"Shoo! Ya lousy thieves!" yelled Boobie.

The monkeys took off and sat at the edge of the stagnant water. One dropped a meal disc into the water and a three-course dinner exploded before him. He screeched with delight, and soon dozens of monkeys lined up at the water's edge where they dipped meal discs into the water. The monkeys jumped up and down every time a disc erupted into huge plates of lasagna or turkey dinners. Little did they care that these meals were nutritional wonders.

"Give them things back to me friends, ya dim-wits!" bellowed Boobie.

The hairy bandits yapped monkey profanities back at Boobie. The primates huddled at the water's edge noshing on their stolen stash of food in spite of Boobie's threats.

"Let's get out o' harm's way," Boobie said. "Them lousy hinks watch ya if yer out here too long."

They all stepped into the bus. As the doors slammed behind Shayna, a monster mosquito smashed into the glass door, short of realizing a feast of her blood.

Boobie started the engine after three tries and then puttered along the jungle road. Monkeys jumped up and clung to whatever parts of the bus were clingable.

One monkey perched on the side-view mirror, picked nits from the hair between her toes, and then ate the wee insects. Yuck! How rude.

Shayna checked the locks on all windows. She didn't want any nit-picking monkeys creeping inside.

Boobie lit a cigar and, within seconds, the interior of the bus was blanketed with a gray fog.

The jungle thinned ahead, allowing Shayna to see a yellow and green savannah through a break in the trees. All the monkeys scurried on top of the bus.

"Hinks ahead," yelled Boobie.

Shayna spotted a herd of repulsive orange-haired creatures racing about the savannah. They were filthy beasts that looked like a cross between woolly mammoths and iguanas. The hink herd galloped straight toward the bus, their massive teeth bared. Long foamy strands of slobber flew from their lips. Their red eyes dominated their faces.

Shayna was certain that everyone was a goner. She almost passed out from the massive amounts of adrenaline rushing through her veins.

"Prepare to excite the herd," said Boobie. He puffed casually on a cigar, remarkably calm given that they were all about to die.

"Why do we need to excite them?" asked Dan. He rummaged around his bottomless pit pockets for the goo grenades. He knew he brought enough grenades to be able to smother the entire hink herd with sticky goo.

"Hinks are narcoleptic," said Boobie. "Ya know, fall asleep when excited."

The monkeys chewed on stolen gumplosion balls and screeched as they blew plump bubbles. Dazzling bubbles popped, spewing tinier bubbles in the direction of the hideous hinks. The thick fog of bubbles blanketed the herd of hinks, and then *whap* ... they all fell over fast asleep.

The monkeys on the roof of the bus stomped in celebration. Shayna jumped up and down, cheering like one of the monkeys.

"I gotta get me some of that there stuff you call candy," said Boobie. Dan handed him a full bag of candy. Boobie stopped the bus, held the bag to his heart, and a tear trickled down his cheek. "Another gift. I ain't ever had such a good day." He wiped his nose and restarted the bus. "I ain't got nothing to give yous, 'cept maybe a rag and some fiberglass resin."

"Helping us is the biggest gift you could give us," said Shayna. She really meant it. Plus, she wasn't too keen on receiving a used rag or fiberglass resin for a gift.

"Ya know, this rescuing of folks is the most fun I ever had," Boobie said. Shayna might have noticed his smile had his teeth, or lack of them, not distracted her.

Boobie drove across the savannah, past a pack of giralephants. The monkeys dismounted the bus at the border of the savannah and sauntered into a forest.

Within seconds, there were large centipedes and millipedes smothering the bus. The sound of millions of legs dragging along the body of the bus was almost unbearable. Boobie drove under hanging shrubbery so that he could clear the window of bugs. Dan wiped his limbs, feeling like creepy-crawlies were on him.

"We're here," said Boobie, once beyond the bugs' bailiwick.

Shayna and Dan smushed their faces against the bus windows to get a better look at the lush rain forest surrounding the bus. Slugs the size of expectant mink glided over decaying tree stumps, leaving behind rivulets of slime. A molting blue and red parrot munched on the corpse of a massive unidentifiable withered insect. Plump orange fruit dangled perilously from tall trees, occasionally smashing to the ground like meteors.

Water dripped with a soothing rhythm from the canopy of trees high above. A three-toed sloth lackadaisically climbed one of the tallest trees near the bus until it disappeared into the leafy cover.

"This here is the entrance to the Caronstie castle dungeons," said Boobie.

"Where?" Dan asked.

"On the other side of that there waterfall is a door that opens when ya say the secret password," Boobie said.

"What's the secret password?" asked Dan.

"Open sesame," said Boobie.

"How original," Shayna said. She rolled her eyes.

"If we go in now, they will have just finished feeding the prisoners. Pea mush and bread crusts today."

Boobie swung open the doors of the bus. Shayna stepped down the bus stairs and promptly landed on her derriere in slug slime. She got up and slipped again. She got up again and fell back into the slime for the third time. The slime covered her from head to toe, causing Dan and Boobie to laugh so hard that they thought they might never stop.

CHAPTER SIXTEEN
The Dungeons

The waterfall stood a hundred feet high and plummeted into a vast pool of shimmering water. Lush ferns and tropical flowers surrounded the pool as though planted by a master gardener.

"Pertty, ain't it," Boobie commented. "Just don't try swimming in there with all them piranhas. I dipped me foot in a few months back to cool off and lost me baby toe. I'll show it to ya someday."

"Cool," said Dan.

Shayna grimaced. "Thanks, but I think I'll pass."

Boobie led his friends along an emerald-green moss path that wound behind the waterfall. The moss was bouncy like a tumbling mat. Shayna took a moment to delight in the frothing falls rushing down beside them on their left and the ruby-red rock on their right. She shivered in the cool mist behind the waterfall.

Two macaws enjoyed frolicking on a rock jutting into the rear of the waterfall. They ruffled their feathers and ran in and out of the splashing water. Both macaws babbled like birdbrains.

Boobie cleared his throat. "Open sesame."

The ruby wall slid sideways, grinding along the stone track. The macaws stopped frolicking, squawked loudly, and flew away, imitating Boobie's voice.

"*Open sesame, open sesame, open sesame,*" the macaws shrieked. Their shrill voices faded as they flew farther away.

Shayna stared beyond the ruby door into a musty stone hallway that was lit with candles mounted on wall sconces. Mounds of hardened wax drippings caked the gray stone floor.

Boobie led them toward the rusty steel door at the end of the corridor.

He pushed the grimy brass handle, and the door creaked open. "Shh." Boobie put a finger to his lips.

They traveled down another long, dim corridor. At the end of the corridor were doors opening to two limestone-walled stairwells, one going up and one heading down.

Boobie whispered, "Falco's insistin' Minnie Maudde finish workin' on an experiment before he kills her. She'll be down in the dungeons. Don't even know if she's been told yet that today's her last."

Boobie padded down the winding stairwell, followed by Shayna and Dan.

"What's the experiment?" Shayna asked.

"Don't know," Boobie shrugged. "It's confidential."

Suddenly, they heard voices at the bottom of the stairs. Someone was coming! Boobie hid with Dan and Shayna behind a nook in the wall. The three stood plastered against the nook, silent as mice, barely breathing.

A sinfully ugly man wearing a scowl ascended the stairs with an equally ugly child. Both had wild frizzy hair.

"Down there is the ones we'll be hangin' today," the ugly man said. "Good to teach ya the ropes, boy. We'll use a 'specially rough one for that lady Terraman, eh."

The boy gave a satisfied grunt.

When the father and son were out of sight, Boobie motioned Dan and Shayna to follow him.

Dan put his hand on Shayna's shoulder. "Go ahead. I've got your back."

If it weren't for Boobie in front of her and Dan behind to protect her, Shayna knew she would probably have been too frightened to move forward. Her legs felt detached from her body. She took a deep breath and somehow forced her wobbly legs to carry her onward.

At the bottom of the stairs, they leaped over foul mud puddles swarming with water mites. Shayna and Dan shadowed Boobie, who led them to a common room encircled by twenty solid iron doors. Above each door, the inhabitant's crime was posted ... crimes like refining sugar, laughing out loud, singing, promoting frivolity, and public smiling. Two signs simply said "Terraman."

In the middle of the common room was a huge heap of unprocessed cotton. Cockroaches scurried under the heap.

"Every day the prisoners must gin cotton for sale to the common public," said Boobie with a hushed tone. "It's the only time they get out of their cells."

A puny window with broad iron bars embellished each cell door. Boobie peeked into one of the cells.

"This here's the kid."

Dan lunged at the window and pushed his face against the bars. What he saw couldn't have been more sickening. A skinny, pale boy was huddled on the damp floor, wearing only a pair of ratty shorts. Dan barely recognized him. He was filthy. The bottoms of his feet were black. His hair was scraggly. Ribs stuck out with each breath to the point that it appeared that they might erupt through his skin. There was nothing in his cell, not even a blanket.

"Sometimes I bring the boy somethin' to play with, like a piece of string or a mouse. But them mice don't like it in there. It's too damp. Sometimes I put old newspapers in there for him to cover up and stay warm. He usually just reads 'em though," said Boobie. "Hey, kid, I brought ya some stuff in me wallet."

Jimmy squinted to see Boobie at the door. Boobie tossed fruit and nuts to him through the bars. Jimmy fumbled for the nuts on the floor.

"We're going to get you out today, Jimmy," said Dan. "Eat as much as you can. Get some strength." Dan threw him a meal disc through the bars.

Jimmy's sallow eyes became the size of golf balls when he saw Dan. "Dan! Get me out. Please don't leave me," pleaded Jimmy, his hoarse voice barely audible.

Boobie led Shayna to the farthest cell.

"This here's Minnie Maudde's cell," Boobie whispered.

Boobie boosted Shayna up on his knee so she could see through the barred window. The cell was packed with various gadgets, test tubes, and bottles filled with brightly colored liquids.

Shayna saw a woman. Minnie Maudde! Boobie smacked his hand over Shayna's mouth when he noticed her about to squeal with excitement.

Minnie Maudde was an incredibly fit woman of indiscernible age. Despite the dust and dirt that plastered her skin, Minnie Maudde was attractive. Her short leather lace-up boots, wool socks folded over the tops, were stylish. Her flowered, knee-length dress was spattered with spots of something black and tar-like. Her golden hair was tied up in a messy bun. Crow's feet marred the edges of her eyes, a sign that captivity had wreaked havoc on her. Minnie Maudde hummed as she alternated between mixing test tubes and writing with a quill on parchment.

Shayna spied a short rotund man with a greasy moustache sitting in a corner of the cell at a small table stacked high with flasks and half-filled test tubes. He had miniscule, beady eyes with no whites. He wore a gray woolen cape that reminded Shayna of wings. He had virtually no nose to speak of. The man's face pointed forward, and he had what seemed to be pale beak-like lips.

Shayna's beating heart smashed against her chest wall and echoed in her ears.

"Falco?" Shayna whispered to Boobie.

Boobie nodded.

Falco bellowed over Minnie Maudde's humming, "Finish the lousy experiment and I promise I will be finished with you. I have no need to keep an old hag like you around."

"You most certainly have no need to keep me around," Minnie Maudde replied. "Except that I'm the only one who can invent the condensed explosive for you. But, gosh, I'm sure you're aware of that, aren't you, bird man?"

"How dare you! You shall call me Your Majesty!" Falco belted. He rose from the table and paced about the makeshift laboratory.

Falco continued, "It's been a month. You still haven't come up with a compact explosive. I'm warning you …"

"What, sonny? You'll kill me? Maybe I'm at the brink of a discovery that could change the way the world looks at you, and you want to end it just hours before I finish! You are insane, wacko, short a few marbles, laughable!"

"That is it! You're done now, you wizened old crow!" Falco shouted. He swiped his arm along the table, smashing any test tubes in his reach. He darted toward the cell door.

Boobie grabbed Shayna and Dan and hoisted them onto the overhead beams just as Falco unlatched the cell door.

Falco turned toward Minnie Maudde and burst with a conniption fit. "I will torture you, hag! You will create that explosive today! And then I will hang you over the cliffs and let the eagles pick out your eyes and organs one by one!"

"Maybe, then, I won't create the explosive until tomorrow," Minnie Maudde said.

Falco practically flew out the door.

Boobie feigned cleaning the cotton pile of dead rats. He picked up the carcasses by the tails and deposited them into a holey bucket. Falco bolted past Boobie without a glance.

Within moments, cheerful humming arose from the lab. Minnie Maudde rearranged the surviving test tubes and peeked through the cell bars. She reached into her sock, pulled out tiny round pellets, and grinned.

"I'll give you your condensed explosive, Falco. Explode this, bird man."

Kaboom!

Minnie Maudde's cell door blasted from its hinges, spraying shards of metal all about. Prisoners in other cells looked out from their wee windows and cheered with gravelly voices. Minnie Maudde straightened her hair, gathered her tattered sweater, and ducked out the destroyed door.

The explosion loosened the beam on which Shayna and Dan were perched. It creaked and then snapped in half, causing Dan and Shayna to slide off and plop onto the heap of cotton. Shayna tumbled down the pile and landed on her buttocks in front of Minnie Maudde. She popped to her feet.

"Hi, I'm Shayna Gladstone. It's nice to meet you."

Shayna stuck out her hand to shake Minnie Maudde's.

"Well, I'll be," said Minnie Maudde. "Shayna Gladstone, you say? I hope your grandfather isn't too hurt that he hasn't heard from me for a while."

"I'm sure he'll understand. He wouldn't hold a kidnapping against you," said Shayna. This was the moment she had waited for. Just one day ago she wasn't sure she would ever be here, talking to Minnie Maudde ... rescuing her.

Minnie Maudde bent down and touched Shayna's face. "Look at you. Such a grown-up girl. And you remind me so much of your mother. Same lips, same eyes, and same strength of character. I'll bet you're even a fantastic mathematician too."

Shanya smiled. "Yeah, I am pretty good at math."

Minnie Maudde laughed and pulled Shayna to her. They shared a hug, and for that brief moment, Shayna felt safe. Boobie couldn't help himself and joined in.

"Dan," said Minnie Maudde. She stepped toward him and clutched him to her heart. "Somehow, I knew I would see you here."

With tears welling up in his eyes, Boobie interrupted, "Sorry to break up this up, but y'all gotta go. The explosion will have wakened Falco's officials, I'm sure." He wiped his nose on his threadbare sleeve.

"We can't leave without Jimmy," insisted Dan.

"Ya won't," said Boobie. "We'll use some of that there explosive to get him out."

Minnie Maudde pulled a handful of pellets from her sock, which obviously boasted a bottomless pit pocket.

"Condensed bat guano," Minnie Maudde informed Boobie as she put a pile of them in his hand. "Two pellets will do the job."

Boobie respectfully saluted Minnie Maudde. Dan handed him a package of voice-activated matches. Boobie placed two pellets and a match on each hinge.

"Ignite," said Dan. The match sparked, and the pellets exploded, shattering the cell door.

Dan ran into the cell and propped Jimmy onto his back.

"Go. Go now," said Boobie. "I'll free everyone else."

"But you're coming too!" said Shayna.

"Me? Ya want me to come with yous?"

"Of course," said Shayna. "We wouldn't leave you here."

"I gotta help these prisoners escape. They ain't done nothin' wrong," said Boobie. "It's the most fun I'll ever have, savin' their lives and all."

"Falco will kill you if he finds out," said Dan.

"Stupid old quack will never know I did it," said Boobie.

"You know I'm not going back to Terramanna without you," said Shayna. "You're my friend."

They all felt the rumbling footsteps of Falco's troops above the dungeons.

"Go! I beg you, me friends," said Boobie. "I'll be right behind you."

"Boobie, you are a saint," said Minnie Maudde. She saluted him, causing Boobie to sob as he ran to free the prisoners.

Dan, piggy-backing Jimmy, led the group out of the common room, through the mud puddles, and along the corridor. The group made their way up to the landing between the sets of winding stairs.

Voices filled the stairwell above. The most prominent voice was Falco's. "If we are lucky, that hag blew herself up with condensed explosive and we won't have to go to the trouble of hanging her tonight."

Falco's men agreed dutifully that such an event would be satisfactory. Falco stopped midway down the stairs to issues his orders. "I know she's not dead. That brainless woman is too smart to have blown herself to pieces.

"Corvus, call the entire city to the Caronstie cliffs for seven o'clock sharp. By my orders, any who don't attend the Terraman's hanging will be whipped and sentenced to life."

"It will be done immediately, Your Majesty." Corvus bowed and hastened back up the stairs.

"Cathartes, as my senior commander, you will have the honor of torturing the hag until six thirty this evening, when you will take her to the gallows on the cliff."

"Thank you, Your Majesty." Cathartes bowed.

"Gavia and Meleagris, you will go with Cathartes. Between tortures, ensure that the hag gives you the recipe for condensed explosives. If you don't get it from her, you will not be leaving the dungeons. Hang the Terraman boy too and display their heads on the stakes at the cliff."

"We will not fail you, Your Majesty," Gavia replied.

"I shall go to my throne room now to prepare the execution speech," said Falco. He stomped up the stairs.

Cathartes lingered with Gavia and Maleagris in the stairwell, discussing various tortures. Minnie Maudde took the opportunity to chew as much stretch gum as she could fit in her mouth.

"Let's hold them off so Boobie can do his thing," Minnie Maudde mumbled as she created huge wads of gum. "We'll use stretch gum to keep them at bay."

Shayna quietly shut the studded door at the bottom of the stairwell in which Falco's cronies loitered. Minnie Maudde and Shayna giggled as they taped the door shut by stretching long strands of stretch gum across the door, wrapping the strand ends around nubby iron spikes sticking out of the walls. This lady was really very fun, Shayna thought.

"That should hold," Minnie Maudde whispered.

The door opened a crack. A hairy hand with blue veins wrapped around Minnie Maudde's wrist. She shrieked and tugged, but the hairy hand tightened its grip. The voices behind the door yelled for Falco. Shayna reached into her bottomless pit pocket and pulled out a gumplosion ball that was larger than an average prehistoric dinosaur egg.

"Ready?" Shayna yelled to Minnie Maudde. She flipped her hair off her shoulder.

Minnie Maudde nodded, anxious to break free.

Shayna approached the door to throw the gumplosion ball and was greeted with Falco's sinister glare from the other side of the widening crack. He scowled at her such that she was certain that if she were on the other side of the door, he would immediately disembowel her with the sword hanging from his belt. Shayna stood frozen. She then gathered her senses. Falco was no match for her.

She whipped the gumplosion ball through the crack of the door. She saw it explode against Falco's forehead into hundreds of smaller gumballs. The door slammed shut.

CHAPTER SEVENTEEN
The Fun Force

Five hours crawled by and Marie had not heard from her friends. True to her word, Marie told the Balloon Lady of the Fun Force plan to rescue Minnie Maudde.

"Why, how can that be any fun whatsoever for those valiant children? It's downright dangerous," said the Balloon Lady as dozens of sour candies tinkled out of her sleeves and dribbled to the floor in front of Marie. "You, my friend, must immediately travel with me to the royal palace, where we can discuss this with the Queens' Council."

At the palace, Marie stood at a podium before the entire Queens' Council. She was so scared to speak in front of the council that her throat dried up and she couldn't think of what to say. She felt her knees might give out. She hated public speaking. Yet the instant she spoke about the Fun Force rescue plans, everyone gave her their undivided attention.

Without delay, the queens, in an attempt to calm their distress, ordered a meal of simmering stews, chili, fajitas, and macaroni with cheese. While eating, the queens took extraordinary measures and coordinated a search-and-rescue team to enter the jungle barrier through the hole in the Hypogeal Park diamond glass wall. Among those appointed to this team were Atlas and Sandy, a massive body builder, a bald-headed monk, Madam Clarissa O'Dell (a psychic whose premonitions were more appropriately termed postmonitions), Ridgley Barnhum-Smythe (the famed circus lion-tamer), and Quinton Albuquerque, commonly known as Terramanna's Minister of War and Peace and Other Fine Literary Works.

Marie knew she had to be on the inside to receive information about what was being done to find Shayna and Dan. So, she insisted that she be appointed the jungle barrier ambassador, in the interest of fun, of course.

The queens agreed that she could have fun being the jungle barrier ambassador, and they also told her that, as ambassador, she had the right to attend all dignitary and council meetings. She had obviously inherited her political talents from her diplomatic mother.

The queens questioned Marie in depth, asking probing questions, such as, "What animals lurk in the jungle? What dangerous plants are there? What is there to eat?"

Marie revealed the dangers of the jungle barrier, causing the queens such fright that they had to adjourn to have a snack of roasted cocoa nibs on cream cheese granola squares. After their snack, the queens ordered the dispatch of the search and rescue team to the jungle barrier.

"Ambassador Marie Dubrand has informed us of the dangers in the jungle," said Queen Beatrix to the search-and-rescue team. "You are authorized to use sticky ammunition in sub-lethal quantities to defend yourself from hinks, blue-barred stinging beetles, and other predators. The children are the priority. May the power of peace and merriment be your guide. Onward to the subterranean jungle!"

Marie watched the search-and-rescue team board the bullet train. The gold train zipped across the Zyluss River in record time.

Marie boarded a crimson train with silver flapping wings bound for Jujube Junction to await news of her friends. When she stepped off the train at Jujube Junction, she was mobbed by a group of kids who were pushing trading cards in her face and asking for her autograph.

"What een the world ..." She sifted through the stack of trading cards handed to her. There were oodles of holographic projection Fun Force trading cards showcasing Shayna, Dan, and herself.

Marie was signing cards when a steam train chugged into the station with the conductor perched on top, holding reins. The Balloon Lady hopped down from the second compartment.

"Don't you simply adore the trading cards?" said the Balloon Lady, waving a stack of cards. "What a resounding success. Created by the palace printers in record time. I got mine at the palace train stop. Oh, please sign mine too. I've swapped six so far. These cards are trading like hotcakes, if you can imagine the enthusiasm with which hotcakes are traded."

Marie was shy about the commotion her presence created on the train platform, so she pushed through the crowd to find some peace. Outside the station, near the towering gummy chew dispensers, she noticed a trading card booth manned by David Johns, the Riff Rafts stopper. A long corral-style line at the booth was packed with people waiting for Fun Force trading cards.

Everyone in the line was negotiating swaps of the trading cards, eating candy-coated chocolate eagles (both plain and peanut), and dancing. Meatballs, the famous scrumption band, entertained the crowd with an impromptu concert from balloons that circled over the queue.

Marie sneaked past the crowd but soon found herself face-to-face with Christie and her clique.

"What is this?" said Christie, shoving a trading card in Marie's face. Christie, MaMoo, and Alexis backed Marie behind a row of lemonade fountains. Marie fell on her rear end. The three girls stood over her.

"Leave me alone or I will tell," said Marie.

"Tell what, French fry?" said Christie. "No one can understand what you say anyway."

"Leave me alone," yelled Marie.

MaMoo and Alexis held Marie's arms and legs, pinning her to the ground. Marie could have easily broken free of their weak grips and slugged them, but she didn't want to beat up smaller girls. She knew she would get in trouble if she did that.

"This stupid trading card says you are an ambassador. Who made you an ambassador? Ambassador of what?"

"None of your business," said Marie.

"Tell me, Frenchy," said Christie. "Or I'll smother you in hasty hardening honey."

"Are you threatening me?"

Christie straddled Marie and pulled a vial from her purse. She uncorked the vial. "No," said Christie. "I wouldn't just threaten you." She tipped the vial and let a stream of honey flow onto Marie's hair. It instantly hardened, causing long strands of Marie's hair to stand on end. The gaggle of girls cackled.

It took all Marie's willpower to hold back from smashing the girls in the face. She knew she would really hurt them if she punched them. They were weaklings.

"You're not an ambassador, are you?" said Christie.

"Eet ees none of your business," said Marie, wrestling against the licorice ropes the girls had tied around her wrists and ankles.

"Fine," said Christie. Christie dripped more and more hasty hardening honey onto Marie until she gave in to the torture.

"Okay," yelled Marie. "You want to know. Eet was the queens. They made me an ambassador. The jungle barrier ambassador. Shayna's Fun Force ees een the jungle barrier. Satisfied?"

"You're a liar," said Christie. "I've never heard of any jungle barrier."

"That ees because you are an eediot."

"Like the queens are going to make you an ambassador. Ambassadors can make orders. You're such a fraud."

Christie dumped the remainder of the hasty hardening honey on Marie, sealing her to the ground lying face up.

"If your stupid Fun Force is in any barrier, they're dead meat, you know," said Christie.

The clique tottered away in their high heels, leaving Marie glued to the ground.

Marie stared at the sky. What choice did she have? She saw the crest of Caronstie hanging above the cliffs. She felt sick to her stomach knowing that Shayna and Dan were alone in the jungle barrier. What if Boobie didn't help them? What if they got caught? What if some of the jungle beasts … arghhh. Christie was right; they were as good as dead.

"'elp," yelled Marie. "Someone 'elp."

David Johns heard his teammate's cries for help and ran to her. He hosed off the hasty hardening honey with a lemonade hose stored behind the fountains. Marie struggled to hold back tears.

"I didn't know hasty hardening honey hurt that much," said David. He untied the licorice ropes.

"Eet ees Dan and Shayna," said Marie. She spilled the whole story to David.

"What eef I waited too long to tell the queens? What eef the search-and-rescue team can't find them?"

"Well, maybe they already found them. Let's check the news," said David. He pulled out his m.a.p.

He looked at Marie and swallowed hard.

"What? What ees eet? What does eet say?"

David read aloud, "By ordinance of the queens, Hypogeal Park is temporarily closed due to the unexpected emergence of aggressive animals known as hinks. It has been determined that these violent hissing hairballs entered Terramanna from Caronstie through a breach in a little-known barrier within the park. The animals attacked a specialized team dispatched by the queens. Minor injuries are reported. The efforts of the queens' team are on hold for up to forty-eight hours as they fight their way through the hink hoards."

There was silence. Marie's heart and mind raced.

"Forty-eight 'ours! We cannot leave them there for another two days. They will never survive a barrier for that long."

"What are you going to do?" asked David.

"What do you mean?"

"Jeesh, Marie," said David. "You *are* an ambassador. You do know what to do, right?"

"The queens just made me an ambassador for fun. I 'ave no idea what to do. Unless ..." The wheels of Marie's mind churned. "Of course. The bats! Why did I not think of eet before? I know exactly 'ow to get eento the jungle. Send a message to the Queens' Council to 'ave the search-and-rescue team meet me at the rafters launch. I know another way eento the jungle."

Marie felt like she was walking on a cloud. Maybe Shayna and Dan wouldn't be dead meat after all.

CHAPTER EIGHTEEN
The Rescue

Dan bolted through the stone corridors with Jimmy on his back. Shayna and Minnie Maudde sprinted behind him.

Kaboom!

"That would be Boobie," Minnie Maudde said. "Thank goodness he's freeing the prisoners. Poor souls aren't long for the world in those conditions, I'm afraid."

They turned around to see the studded door opening. Then, with a loud snap, the door slapped shut. The gum was working as they had hoped. There was a load of commotion behind the door, including repeated falling on the gumballs. Gumball rainbows spewed through the door crack. Again the door opened and then snapped shut. And again. Shayna knew that the gum wouldn't hold much longer.

Another explosion from the dungeons rocked the floors. And yet another shattered the air, blowing an iron door from its hinges and down the corridor.

They lingered short of the exit, looking back. A gray cloud of dust rolled through the corridor.

"Where is he?" yelled Shayna. She started back down the corridor to get Boobie just as his figure burst through the wall of dust.

"Run!" shouted Boobie. "Run!"

Falco's men poked large serrated blades through cracks and cut at the gum. Shayna's heart pounded. It was only a matter of seconds before the torturers would completely slash away the stretch gum.

"*Open sesame*," Dan yelled as he raced to the door with Jimmy on his back. They hustled through the ruby doorway just as a massive explosion roared throughout the corridor. The rock crumbled at their backs. They all tumbled to the ground at the edge of the waterfall. Dust billowed around them.

Shayna's clothes were tattered. Her arms and back were bruised and cut. Her body ached all over.

Thunderous crashing of rock inside the corridors continued to pepper the air. Dust sprinkled down around the group. Shayna ripped a sleeve off her shirt and tied it around a deep cut on Dan's leg. Minnie Maudde popped to her feet as though nothing had happened and attended to Jimmy, who was groaning.

Shayna became frantic. "Where's Boobie? Where is he?!"

The two macaws flew to their favorite spot behind the waterfall and sat on the pile of rubble. Boobie's arms and head stuck out from under the pile. The birds mostly mumbled unintelligibly to one another, but now and then squawked, "Open sesame."

CHAPTER NINETEEN
JUNGLE BOUND

David Johns was what some would call a miracle worker. In less than eleven minutes, he managed to gather the Queens' Council and the search-and-rescue team at the rafters launch. In addition, David took the initiative to assemble all of the Riff Rafts, a junior *Sweet Read* reporter by the name of Mohamed Grant, and the Balloon Lady (who heard about this gathering through the grapevine, literally).

Marie's heart thumped hard in her chest. Again, she would have to address the queens, and just the thought of it made her hands shake. She stood with a megaphone at the top of the launch.

"As jungle barrier ambassador, I thank you for joining me 'ere. And thank you to David Johns for assembling you all at this meeting. I called you 'ere to tell you that there ees another entrance to the jungle. Eet ees een a rafters tunnel."

Questions flew from the gathering. "Where?"

"How do you know?"

"Who reported this?"

"How can you be sure?"

"As most of you know, Shayna was een the jungle barrier by mistake. She described seeing bats there, 'orrible, 'uge bats. Then, yesterday I saw bats. And Lars Shermann saw bats. But Lars and I saw them een a tunnel."

Someone in the crowd shouted, "There have been no bats in Terramanna for four hundred years!"

"Four 'undred and fifty-eight. That ees right," said Marie. "Do you understand? The bats Lars and I saw are coming from Caronstie through the tunnels."

The crowd was silent.

"Oh, for goodness sake," said Marie, frustrated. "Shayna's m.a.p. told us there ees an entrance to Caronstie somewhere een the mid-range rafters tunnels. This ees where the bats 'ave been seen. You see, I 'ave now thought about the location of the subterranean jungle een comparison to the tunnels, and I can tell eet lies beneath the mid-range rafters tunnels that sweep below to the south edge of Lake Orange. The bats we saw must be jungle bats. There must be a 'ole somewhere een the mid-range tunnels eento Caronstie."

To clarify her point, Marie drew, on the launch chalk board, a sketch of the tunnels over Hypogeal Park and the jungle.

"Exactly where in the tunnels is this entrance, kiddo?" asked Atlas.

"Well … I do not know for sure. I never saw eet," said Marie.

The crowd groaned.

"But this ees the tunnel where we saw the bats," said Marie, pointing to one of the lines on her drawing. "I am certain that finding the tunnel entrance to the jungle will be much faster than fighting off the 'inks."

"Ambassador Dubrand, with all due respect," said Queen Haspa, "there is no documented evidence of this entrance you speak of. We are wasting valuable time here. Search-and-rescue team, return to Hypogeal Park."

"Wait!" said Marie with the megaphone pressed to her lips. "Documented or not, I know I am right. You must believe me."

Queen Haspa looked ready to explode at Marie—that is, until Sandy spoke. Then she looked ready to explode at him.

"Honorable Queen Haspa," said Sandy. "We need to accept the probability of the existence of such an entrance. Alex Gladstone reported that Sarah fell through such a hole into the jungle only ten years past. Marie is right. It exists."

"Gladstone?" asked Marie.

"There is no clear m.a.p. post recording the existence of this opening," said Queen Haspa. "You and your friends were careless. You did not adhere to the laws. There are procedures, rules, and regulations for a purpose. You and your friends felt above those laws, and they paid with their lives. That is your punishment."

Sandy's jaw hung. Never before had he been admonished like this, let alone by a queen, and in public. He felt like he could crawl under a rock and die.

The Balloon Lady climbed to the top of the launch with a megaphone in hand. Her grass skirt blew in the wind. "If there is the possibility of a quicker route to Caronstie, Queen Haspa, are we not bound by the constitution to investigate that route in the interest of saving the lives of the children? It is my duty as Balloon Lady to ensure children have fun. No fun can be found in a barrier, facing death. Fun is the oath under which I was sworn, and I must speak in honor of this oath."

The crowd was still. In all of recorded history, no one had ever spoken against a queen in this manner.

Queen Haspa drew a deep breath before she spoke. "There are three dignitaries who have now spoken against me. My twin and I must therefore, by law, consider the possibility that my decision is flawed, and we must weigh your comments before making a final binding determination."

Queens Haspa and Beatrix retired to the royal carriage. No one dared make any noise, except the Balloon Lady, of course, who requested from Sandy his recipe for soursop turnovers.

Moments later, the twin queens exited the carriage and stood facing the crowd. Queen Haspa spoke. "I am swayed by the loss of Jimmy Chow in the tunnels two months past. Samosby's report to the council was clear. There is no person skilled enough to navigate the remote mazes throughout the tunnels and find their way back."

"I am," said Marie before she had thought about the consequences of speaking.

The crowd drew a collective breath.

"Correct she is," said Sandy. He already felt demoralized by Queen Haspa's previous comment about him. So he sensed no need to hold back. What more could she do to him? "Marie is the one person who could guide us through the tunnels. She has a unique talent. Yes, a magnificent sense of direction. Best I've ever seen. There is no better choice of leader."

"I was thinking I could just draw a detailed map," said Marie. "I did not mean …"

"Is Ambassador Dubrand skilled enough?" interrupted Queen Beatrix. "We shall put it to a vote. Raise your hand if you believe reigning junior national rafter champion sneak, Ambassador Marie Dubrand, is highly skilled enough to lead the team in the tunnels."

Every hand in the crowd shot up, except Marie's and Queen Haspa's.

"But, the bats. I am scared of the …" Marie tried to speak for herself but was elected for the job before she knew it.

The Balloon Lady clapped and jawbreakers flew from her sleeves. She declared that, though she wasn't officially a member of the search and rescue team, she must tag along in order to "keep it fun," so to speak.

"What about the bats?" Mohamed Grant asked. He had his pencil perched on his pad of paper, hoping to record a news item worthy of a big investigative reporting award, possibly even a Nobel Prize. "If there are bats in the tunnels, how will you deal with them, ambassador?"

Marie didn't know what to say. Luckily, David Johns stepped forward to speak for her. "There were only two or three bats reported. That's no big deal."

"Will we have anything to eat?" asked Riff Raff member, Calvin Gonzalez.

"We?" said Atlas.

"Yes, the whole team is going with Marie. We all want to be a part of this Fun Force," said Calvin.

"Onward Fun Force!" shouted the Balloon Lady as she pumped Marie's hand in the air.

Tremendous commotion ensued. Everyone grabbed a donut, paddle, life-jacket, and helmet, and launched within record time.

Feeling she had no choice, Marie assumed her elected role and led the Fun Force into a spiraling branch off the level three tunnels. Just as she had reported earlier, the water appeared to flow upward despite the fact that their stomachs told them they were traveling downward.

They meandered past three branches off the spiral and then approached a dark hole in the tunnel wall. Everyone crowded at the entrance of the cramped tunnel and stared into the darkness. Their helmet lights struggled to pierce the velvety blackness. There was hardly any everglow rock in the tunnel, just one vein that faded into the darkness.

"Well, this ees eet. This ees where the bats were," Marie whispered.

No one made a peep. It was so quiet that the only sound was the collective breathing of the group. Marie clenched her paddle, took a deep breath, and was first to move her donut forward into the tight passageway. She dropped tracing lights into the water and they sank to the bottom, leaving a submerged trail of lights behind them as they forged on. She made a chalk line along the stone wall every fifty feet to mark their path.

Beyond a hair-pin turn, the passageway opened into a wider tunnel. Glow rock spattered along the walls dimly lit the path.

Marie heard a massive bat winging overhead, screamed, and ducked in her donut.

As quickly as the bat had appeared, it was gone. When everyone summoned the nerve to uncover their heads and look up, they saw the Balloon Lady standing on her donut, admiring a gargantuan dangling bat.

"My word, you are a handsome bat, as far as bats are concerned," the Balloon Lady said. "Would you kindly advise any further of your hairy comrades to refrain from flitting about in such a flighty manner? Thank you, bat friend. And we shall do our best not to disturb you. That being said, we would be most appreciative if you and your chiroptera camp would return to Caronstie. Thank you and good day."

She sat back down in her donut and noticed everyone watching her. "Oh, goodness. Pardon my dalliance, all. I thought it best to address the bat at this juncture. He is, in fact, a bat sympathetic to our concerns, it would seem."

"'e ees?" said Marie. She eyed the creepy creature dangling from the craggy ceiling, plunged her paddle in the water, and forged ahead.

The team spiraled down two hundred feet, and then the tunnel broke into four tributaries. Marie stopped paddling and examined the direction each tunnel flowed. She drew a map on the wall with chalk.

"Aha!" she said out loud. She rubbed out one of the chalk lines and then drew a different pathway on the map.

With his headlamp switched on, Atlas studied the map, shaking his head. "Wow!" Atlas was flabbergasted with Marie's sense of direction.

"This way," said Marie to the team as she pointed toward the only tributary that was lit with glow rock.

Marie swerved left, laboring to fit her donut around a sharp turn. She found herself perched at the top of the longest tunnel waterfall she had ever seen. She waited for the team and then, one by one, they each plummeted into a still pond at the base of a ten-foot-high granite passageway. Half of the rescue team toppled from their donuts, unable to stay upright.

Bright light emanated from the opening at the top of the vertical corridor. A bat swooped, causing screams to erupt from the crowd, except of course the Balloon Lady, who appeared to rather enjoy the company of the creature.

Marie climbed the rock face and climbed into a massive cave. She was awestruck. “Mon dieu!”

Marie leaned over the ledge of the rock face. “Throw your donuts up ’ere. You will not believe this.” Her voice echoed.

They all tossed their donuts to Marie and then scrambled up the rock face. The team found themselves standing at the threshold of a massive cave.

“Magnificent,” said Mohamed, snapping photos.

Everglow rock lined the entire domed chamber. The rock glowed so intensely that the light it shed could have been mistaken for a passage to heaven.

Multitudes of glittering white stalactites hung from the ceiling, and some touched the colossal stalagmites rising up from the floor, creating mammoth shining pillars. Clusters of dazzling rose quartz crystals spotted the ceiling like stars in the night sky. A green lake sparkled at the far end of the cave. The immense chamber smelled like hard-boiled eggs.

With a sudden clap, a geyser exploded massive volumes of water high into the air. The geyser spouted for at least twenty seconds. The water trickled down flat slabs of everglow rock that descended like stairs into the lake.

A creek snaked from the far end of the lake through a skinny slit of an everglow tunnel.

“Very careful we must be,” said Sandy. “The rock floor is possibly thin and may not be stable. Be sure to tie off on pillars.”

“What are we looking for?” asked Ridgely Barnhum-Smythe.

"An opening into the jungle," said Sandy. "Likely in the floor."

Everyone did their own thing in hopes of finding the opening. The Balloon Lady poked a stick in front of her, testing the stability of the ground while eating a cheese and potato sandwich. Rafter Magnum Dragnall, a young Sherlock Holmes look-alike, searched for clues using his massive magnifying glass. David Johns scoured the floor on his hands and knees.

"Oh no," said Marie. Her face went white. "Eet ees Jimmy's donut. Or what ees left of eet." She held up a chunk of a chocolate rafters donut with mint sprinkles, Jimmy's trademark donut. She felt a lump growing in her throat and would have cried then and there had the geyser not erupted a mere four feet from her. Freaked out, she ran through the slit tunnel.

Before anyone else could make it through the skinny tunnel, Marie yelled, "I found eet. I found the opening!"

Everyone squeezed through the slit and stood around a hole just big enough for a person to fit through. A faded green jacket covered one edge of the hole.

"I knew it would be here," said Madam Clarissa O'Dell.

The *Sweet Read* reporter, Mohamed, snapped a picture of Sandy with the jacket and Marie holding the donut chunk.

A bat as big as a hawk fluttered out of the opening and headed into the large chamber.

"That ees four!" said Marie. "There are four of them. Yuck. Yuck. Yuck. Yuck!"

"Lucky four," said the Balloon Lady. She popped the rest of her sandwich into her mouth.

"Speaking of good fortune," said the Balloon Lady, leaning over the hole, "I can see through the tree canopy. It looks like we're only a scant eight hundred and forty inches from the jungle floor."

Miguel Timber, a stocky rafter, pulled a retractable stretch ladder out of his bottomless pit backpack and secured it around two stalactites. "Well?" He looked to their leader for guidance.

"Let us do eet," said Marie.

"Onward, Fun Force!" cheered the Balloon Lady, using the frayed ends of her fruit ribbon scarf as pompoms.

The entire team scurried down the ladder and found themselves standing on the moss path approaching the waterfall.

"This place is creepy," said David. "Yuck, what is this thing?" A monster mosquito poked at his helmet. He swatted at it. "Ugh, get away!"

Mosquitoes swarmed the Fun Force search-and-rescue team, causing most of them to run around in circles like lunatics, swatting at the beastly bugs.

Without warning, carnivorous plants snatched two of the largest mosquitoes and Madam Clarissa O'Dell in her entirety.

Amanda Owanda, known as the finest junior recoverer, and the Balloon Lady lured the man-eating plant with cinnamon sticks to free the psychic. Suddenly the stalk of the plant stretched and burst open, spilling Madam Clarissa O'Dell onto the dirt.

"No one could have seen that coming!" said Clarissa.

"Precisely," said the Balloon Lady. She fed the plant a sticky bun and it burped.

Mohamed snapped pictures of the carnivorous plant and its disoriented slimy snack.

A heavy wall of dust rolled toward the group.

Dan limped out through the dust from behind the waterfall. "Oh! It's … how did you all … Marie! Help us back here. Please hurry!"

The entire Fun Force ran behind the waterfall. They were met with the sight of Shayna and Minnie Maudde heaving rocks from a pile, and their lost comrade, Jimmy, splayed on the dirt.

"It's Boobie," yelled Shayna to Marie.

"Dig 'im out!" Marie ordered.

Everyone jumped into action and lifted rocks and debris off of Boobie. The Balloon Lady's sleeves sprayed cinnamon hearts as she tossed rocks from the pile. The bodybuilder and Atlas struggled to remove the heavy boulder trapping Boobie's legs.

Boobie lifted his head and whispered. Shayna put her ear next to his mouth. He whispered again.

"I can't hear you, Boobie," said Shayna. "Can you talk any louder?"

She dipped her ear back toward his lips. Her eyes widened.

"Beetles!" Shayna yelled. "Stampede!"

The distant rumble grew louder.

Marie shouted out commands to everyone. Within seconds, the epicurean cannons were set up. The Balloon Lady manned the cannons, which was a job she enjoyed immensely. Others held goo grenades and syrup super sprayers … and tested them for the sake of fun when encouraged by the Balloon Lady. Shayna spread sacs of sugar cement on the ground near the waterfall to create a barrier from the beetles. She accidentally stepped into the sugar cement and lost her shoe in the concoction.

The stampede of blue-barred stinging beetles thundered past the waterfall. The ground shook like an earthquake of cataclysmic proportion.

A handful of lumbering beetles peeked behind the waterfall to see the potential feast of humans. The beetles grunted, kicked their rear legs, and raced toward the Fun Force.

"Fire!" shouted Marie.

The Balloon Lady fired the epicurean cannon and made a direct hit, causing a coyote-sized beetle to slither away, dragging its sticky legs along the ground. The goo grenades and syrup super sprayers took care of the all the remaining beetles but one, which Ridgely Barnhum-Smythe calmly directed away from the scene with meaty treats.

Atlas heaved the largest boulder from Boobie's right leg. Minnie Maudde fished around in her bottomless pit sock pocket and pulled out a complete medical kit. She splinted Boobie's leg and gently braced his neck.

Altas flew Boobie above his head on a makeshift stretcher into the tree canopy and through the hole.

Dan secured Jimmy to his back and climbed the ladder with ease.

On Marie's orders, everyone scurried up the ladder, narrowly escaping a herd of hideous hissing hinks.

CHAPTER TWENTY
BEYOND THE BARRIER

The group was exhausted. Most, including Shayna, rested on the cave floor while Marie scribbled her recollection of the tunnels on a scrap of paper. She swatted at Dan when he suggested corrections to her drawings.

"I know there ees a way out other than climbing the rock going back the way we came. That would be tough to do with Boobie on a stretcher," said Marie.

"And getting around all those waterfalls would be … whew," said Atlas, his lisp heavy.

"Ah, yes, see 'ere." Marie pointed at her drawing.

Dan and Atlas hovered over the drawing.

"What?" said Atlas. "See what?"

"Right 'ere," said Marie, pointing at a line on her sketch. "This part 'ere ees going to have a gentle slope back to the lower section of Lake Orange. Yep, I am sure of eet."

Dan and Atlas looked at each other, amazed.

"Any idea what she's talking about, kiddo?" said Atlas to Dan.

"Not at all," said Dan. "But I trust her."

While waiting for Marie to devise a plan to safely exit the tunnels, some of the rescue team had nodded off, propped up against the stalactite columns. Others sat in groups, talking. Jimmy devoured lasagna, and Minnie Maudde sat cross-legged on her sweater, putting plant samples from her pocket on microscope slides. The Balloon Lady entertained everyone with a peculiar rendition of the River Dance. Wafer cookies flew from her sleeves with every step and made a melodic tapping sound when they fell to the ground.

Shayna sat up. "Quiet everyone," she shouted. She put a finger up. "What's that screeching?"

"Bats," said Boobie, half in and out of consciousness.

Suddenly the largest colony of bats in the history of imagination invaded the cave. Deafening flapping echoed throughout the arched chamber. Horrific high-pitched squeals filled every space of air. Racing at the Fun Force was a wall of king-sized bats.

"*Duck!*" Marie yelled.

"They ain't no ducks," mumbled Boobie.

Shayna slipped on wet rock near the geyser and skidded along the smooth everglow rock on her rear end. Within seconds, she was speeding feet-first through hundreds of hairy bats. She screamed as the bats skimmed along her body and whipped around her ponytail.

When the squealing faded, there was no sound but the Irish music blaring from the Balloon Lady's m.a.p.

Shayna lay paralyzed on the floor for what seemed like an hour. She gathered the nerve to open one eye and saw the bats had vanished from the cave into the jungle.

Marie remained curled up on the ground like a lump.

"They're gone," Shayna whispered. "The bats are gone."

Marie raised her head and looked around. She gasped for air as though she hadn't breathed at all since the ordeal began, and quite possibly hadn't.

"We 'ave 'ad enough fun for one day," said Marie. "Someone cover that 'ole eento the jungle. We are going 'ome."

CHAPTER TWENTY - ONE

Home

Shayna, Dan, and Marie sat side by side on mushroom stools near lemonade fountains while they binged on fresh buttered popcorn at the base of the erupting popcorn volcano.

"The roots of the lemon trees supply the lemon flavor to the fountain," said Dan. "The citric acid is absorbed—"

"I see you are back to normal, Mr. Know-Eet-All," said Marie.

The perpetual clock struck three.

"It's time," said Shayna. "Let's get to the palace."

They ran to Jujube Junction, where they handed the Ploomi conductor their banana leaf tickets to board the peppermint-winged royal train.

Marie pulled the *Sweet Read* out of the seat pocket and read the article written by Mohamed. Splashed on the front page was Shayna's m.a.p. picture, tripping nonetheless, under the headline, "Shayna's Fun Force Breaks Barrier." A second picture showed Dan hauling Jimmy up the ladder.

"Look 'ere. You two are 'eroes," said Marie.

"So are you, Ambassador Dubrand. A hero, that is." Shayna pointed at the second paragraph of the newspaper article and read, "Ambassador Marie Dubrand relied on her extraordinary spatial sense and innate leadership skills to guide nineteen Fun Force search-and-rescue members successfully through uncharted tunnels to the jungle barrier."

"Sweet," said Marie.

The crystal mint chandeliers tinkled as the train chugged along.

Shayna continued reading. "A team of animal trainers headed by Ridgely Barnhum-Smythe has successfully herded the hinks back into the jungle. The hole in the diamond glass wall is undergoing extensive repairs. Hypogeal Park will reopen on Thursday to those who can figure out how to get in."

The train came to a full stop, and the passengers exited by sliding down the minty wings to the platform.

When they hit the platform, star-struck fans demanded that they autograph trading cards.

Shayna was hit in the forehead by an errant paper airplane. She picked it up and unfolded it. It was a Shayna Number Thirteen card with a handlebar moustache drawn on with black marker. She heard cackling behind her and turned to see Christie run behind a pillar.

"Get her!" shouted a black-haired boy, pointing at Christie. He and three other boys cornered her.

"Hey, what are you doing?" screamed Christie.

"Don't ever wreck those cards again. That was a Shayna Number Thirteen. That card is rare," said the boy.

"I'll do what I want," said Christie.

The boys held Christie against the pillar.

"Okay, blondie. Just to prove our point …" said the black-haired boy. He drew a thick moustache on Christie's face with black magic marker.

Christie shrieked and ran away through the crowd, screaming. Marie snorted.

Drums beat to signal the start of the parade. Leading the parade was a scrumption band in flashy uniforms. Following them were twenty Gomock clowns, the queens in a gilded carriage, and Minnie Maudde with Jimmy on a delicious float made entirely of peanut brittle. A score of double-jointed acrobats followed. Much of Shayna's Fun Force rode in miniature orange balloons with green and red swirls. Shayna, Dan, and Marie waved to the crowd from the basket of a balloon that flashed scenes from their adventures in the jungle, as recorded by Mohamed. The final and most elaborate float carried Boobie, who didn't stop sobbing with joy the entire parade.

At the end of the parade, fireworks exploded from the top of the palace. As the fireworks reached their pinnacle in the sky, they broke open and sprinkled a kaleidoscope of red-apple-flake confetti on everyone below.

The Fun Force gathered on the Palace Terrace, which overlooked all of Terramanna. Shayna stopped at the railings with her two friends to look down at Cookie Corner just to the east of Marshmallow Meadow. Dan pointed out the Hot Fudge Toboggan Hill, Caramel Cove, Almond Alley, and the Nut Factory, where he claimed Falco must have been born.

Chimes sounded, and everyone took a seat on the terrace. Boobie pushed through the crowd on his crutches to find a chair next to Shayna.

The Balloon Lady stood on a platform made of dehydrated kiwi fruit, pink grapefruit, pomegranates, and papayas. "Could I have your attention, please? Thank you." She shooed a red-headed woodpecker from her tall foliage hat before continuing. "We are gathered here for a fantastic ceremony, a citizenship ceremony to be certain. Mr. Boobie Schumpert, we welcome you as Terramanna's newest and much adored citizen."

Boobie rose to his feet and hobbled along a carpet of granola to the platform. Queen Beatrix draped a sparkling sugar medal around Boobie's neck while Queen Haspa handed him a scroll certifying him as a citizen of Terramanna, along with his very own m.a.p.

Shayna led a standing ovation, which caused Boobie to weep and wipe his nose on the sleeve of his new plaid shirt.

"Have you any words you'd like to say, Mr. Schumpert?" asked the Balloon Lady. She handed him a gumdrop-studded microphone.

"Uh, well, uh, I ain't never spoken in public before," said Boobie. "But, uh, well, I guess I'd like to say that I ain't never had a friend before I met Shayna on me Jungle Ryde Tour. Now look how many friends I gots. All 'cause o' her.

"I'd like to thank Shayna fer the funnest time I ever did have. And I never knew bein' free could be so much fun. Thank you."

"Precisely," said the Balloon Lady. "That leads nicely into my next topic: Shayna of the Prophecy and her Fun Force."

The entire audience clapped on cue.

"Though it is questionable whether it could be fun being in a barrier, it has been determined that no constitutional laws have been broken by the Fun Force. Fun is sometimes a process. And as long as Shayna's efforts foster fun, especially fun for others, such as the likes of Mr. Boobie Schumpert, we support her efforts to create a Fun Force that will conquer all gloom. Mr. Schumpert is having fun. And I know I'm having fun. What about the rest of you?"

The entire crowd chanted, "Fun, fun, fun!"

There wasn't one television or radio that wasn't tuned into the Balloon Lady's speech. People in every restaurant, every home, every store, and every nook and cranny cheered for the Fun Force and its leader, Shayna of the Prophecy.

"The Age of Gloom is upon us," the Balloon Lady continued. "We still have much work to do to protect our precious lands from Falco's army of gloom. Caronstie may have declared war against us, but we remain committed to a peaceful resolution to the conflict. Terramanna will not use violence against Caronstie. We will use a greater force … Fun! Fun! Fun!" She twirled in circles, spraying mini chocolate chip cookies from her sleeves.

The crowd cheered. "Fun! Fun! Fun!"

"Let the party begin!" shouted the Balloon Lady.

The beating of drums began, and the Meatballs started their concert from balloons circling over Terramanna. People everywhere were dancing in the streets. Scrumptions flew about, cheering and blowing horns.

Shayna stood on the palace terrace, overlooking Terramanna. This was the biggest party she could ever imagine.

"Lovely view, isn't it?" said Minnie Maudde.

"Oh, I didn't see you there," said Shayna with a start. "I bet you're happy to be home."

"I most certainly am," said Minnie Maudde. "But, you know, I truly did have moments of great joy in the dungeons. I became friends with many of the prisoners. And you can't imagine the fun I had creating new inventions with primitive tools in prison. Come now, bat poop explosives. What a marvelous creation! And I loved taunting Falco into believing I was working on condensed explosives all that time, but I actually came up with the recipe on my second day there."

Shayna laughed. "What were you doing the rest of the time?"

"Oh, that was the really fun part. See what I made?" Minnie Maudde pulled a paper-thin blue feather from her bottomless pit purse. "I call these flutterfuns."

Minnie Maudde released a flutterfun above their heads. It glided through the air in circles, giggling until it disintegrated into scented dust.

"They're fantastic!" said Shayna. She was proud that someone as brilliant as Minnie Maudde was her relative.

"I left thousands of flutterfuns in Caronstie in the pockets of everyone who came into the dungeons … even Falco," said Minnie Maudde. "Just imagine what will happen when these flutterfuns get lifted on the wind." Minnie Maudde laughed so hard that she had to hold her stomach.

Despite the frivolity, Shayna wished she was with her grandfather. She leaned on the terrace railing and sighed. An exciting tension welled up in her. Finally, she could ask Minnie Maudde to find a way for her to get home.

"What is it?" asked Minnie Maudde.

"I want to go home. I miss my grandfather." Shayna turned and looked straight into Minnie Maudde's eyes. "Will you find a way for me to get back through the IDL hole?"

"Hmm, let me think." Minnie Maudde scratched her temple and took a deep breath. "Well, it will take my scientific team some time to create a cloaking system for balloons. But that's something we've wanted to do for a while, anyway. Then, of course, we will have to penetrate Falco's defenses at the IDL hole. He certainly will be building a barrier there as we speak."

"Why don't you just blast Falco's armies with some explosives?" asked Shayna.

"My dear, Terramans do not resort to violence. Violence and fun are incompatible."

"But you can get me home, right?"

"Of course. Of course, I could find a way," said Minnie Maudde. "But is that what you really want?"

"What do you mean?"

"Shayna, my dear, this is your home," said Minnie Maudde. "Don't you know? You were born here. You are a Terraman."

"Pardon me?"

"Yes, dear. Your parents raised you here until the day they died," said Minnie Maudde. "I've missed you so much. When you and your grandfather left Terramanna, you were the cutest little thing, just learning to talk."

Shayna's eyes grew wide. "No one ever told me that I was born here."

Shayna didn't know how she was supposed to feel. She was shocked. She felt numb. She felt deceived.

"Why didn't Grandpa tell me?" said Shayna.

"My dear," said Minnie Maudde, "he loves you. He would do anything to protect you from pain, perhaps even if that meant protecting you from your destiny."

A Tympocki *Sweet Read* science reporter flew toward Minnie Maudde, bobbing up and down with the weight of the camera on his shoulder. He tapped Minnie Maudde on the arm.

"Please think about it before you decide what you really want," said Minnie Maudde, and she spun around to start her interview with the reporter.

"Decide? What are you deciding?" said the Balloon Lady, who seemed to appear out of thin air. She offered Shayna a piece of lime cake piled high with velvety whipped cream frosting.

"Minnie Maudde asked me to think about whether I really want to go back home … back to my grandfather."

"You are home," said the Balloon Lady. "Oops, putrefied peach pits. I shouldn't have said anything." The Balloon Lady covered her mouth with both hands and mimed locking her lips with an imaginary key.

"I already know," said Shayna. "Minnie Maudde told me I was born here."

"Oh, thank goodness it wasn't me who spilled the beans," said the Balloon Lady, unlocking her lips. "Yet I do find it remarkable how you're carrying on with the work your parents started, don't you?"

"What do you mean?"

"I mean how they dedicated their lives to rescuing Caronsties from Falco's reign of treachery. Likewise, you rescued Minnie Maudde, Jimmy, and Mr. Boobie Schumpert from Falco's venomous grip. Quite unlike you, however, your parents died in the barriers in their efforts to impart fun on others."

"What?" Shayna's knees crumpled and she almost fell over. "In barriers …"

"Yes, and then you just waltz through the very barrier that your mother died in. Gracious me! She would be so proud of you for pursuing what she and your father started. And so proud that you stood up to Falco like you did."

Shayna stood with her mouth agape, speechless.

"Oh, rotten rutabagas!" The Balloon Lady smacked her forehead. "I can't believe I blurted all that."

Shayna stumbled to the edge of the terrace. Tears rolled down her cheeks. She kicked the juice fountain and banged on the railing with her fists. "I hate you, Falco. My parents died because of you. I hate you!"

She fell to her knees on the grass and stared out over Terramanna, tears streaming down her cheeks.

Dan noticed Shayna alone, crying. He sat down on the grass, facing Shayna, not knowing what to say to make her feel better.

Marie tapped Shayna on the shoulder.

"What ees wrong?" asked Marie. "You are crying."

Marie plopped down on the grass and put her arm around Shayna. "What ees eet?"

Marie looked at Dan and he shrugged.

Shayna shut her eyes tightly. She couldn't even begin to imagine what had happened to her parents in the barriers. She never wanted to know.

"For the first time in my life, my parents are real to me. I never knew what happened to them. My grandfather never wanted to talk about it. But now I know. Now I know they were good people trying to do good things when they died."

"Of course they were good people," said Dan.

"Yes, but, you don't understand," said Shayna. "They died trying to help the Caronsties. The Balloon Lady told me. And she told me how proud my mother would be of me for standing up to Falco."

"I do understand. Believe me," said Dan.

"Your parents lived 'ere?" asked Marie.

Shayna nodded. "All this time I've wanted nothing more than to go home, and now I want nothing more than to stay. This is the closest I'll ever get to my parents. I have to try to finish what they started. I can't go now."

Dan smiled. He understood.

"What about your grandfather?" asked Marie.

"I miss him so much," said Shayna. "But he always told me that I was meant for big things. I think he's always known that this is my destiny."

Dan grabbed Shayna and Marie's hands. "O*ur* destiny," he said.

"*Our* destiny," repeated Marie.

Shayna smiled at her friends, the best friends she could ever imagine. Dan winked at Shayna, and she blushed. Marie snorted.

They raised their linked hands in the air. "Fun Force!"

The popcorn volcano exploded, sending an avalanche of popcorn tumbling down the side of the mountain with wafts of butter scent. The Meatballs balloons drifted over their heads, leaving musical notes dancing on the warm air. The sun was setting over Lake Orange, creating brilliant streaks of color in the sky.

The three friends linked arms and ran toward the festivities. It was going to be a great party indeed.